Stern fears Deena is much like what her sister was.

"I'm not like that. I'm not!"

Did she protest too much? wondered Stern. *Lord, what do I say? Is Deena an innocent and how can I know for sure?*

"I'd like to believe you, Deena, but—"

Tears trickled down Deena's face. "I should have known you wouldn't believe me," she whispered. "My sister must have hurt you dreadfully for you to hold me in such distrust."

Awkwardly, Stern put his arm about her, letting her cry. Wonderingly, Stern stroked the hair that eddied about Deena's shaking shoulders like molten star shine.

He had no idea how long he held her against him, surrounding her with his warm comfort. The girl warmed a piece of his heart, hardened with past hurts and cynicism. If only he could be sure of her. If only he could be sure she was different from Lizzy.

Deena cried until all her tears were spent. Slowly she relaxed in the warmth and security of Stern's arms.

Finally Deena pushed herself away from her guardian. Instantly, Stern released her. Looking up, Deena beheld the smile of genuine concern on lips. With his thumb, he wiped a large tear from her cheek. "Feel better?"

"I think so," she whispered. Suddenly she noticed his damp linen shirt, the stained black satin evening jacket. "Oh, dear, I've ruined your clothes!"

With his hand he gathered her long hair off her shoulders. "There are more important things than clothes."

CAROLYN R. SCHEIDIES makes her home in Nebraska with her husband Keith and their two children. Carolyn is active in her church's puppet ministry as well as the pro-life movement. She writes inspirational romance because "what better way to help someone know God's love than through the eyes of characters who live it."

Books by Carolyn R. Scheidies

In Lizzy's Image

Carolyn R. Scheidies

Heartsong Presents

This book is dedicated to my LovKnot & HeartWrite Sisters.

You help keep me on track not only with my writing, but also in my faith walk.

Thanks for all the prayer, support, and encouragement.

A note from the author:
I love to hear from my readers! You may correspond with me by writing:

Carolyn R. Scheidies
Author Relations
PO Box 719
Uhrichsville, OH 44683

ISBN 1-57748-338-3

IN LIZZY'S IMAGE

Cover illustration by Lauraine Bush.

PRINTED IN THE U.S.A.

prologue

Flipping back her long, silvery blond hair, Deena frowned at her image in the mirror. In the worn gown of mourning black, she looked far too young, far too vulnerable for her nineteen years.

With the deaths of first her mother and now her father, the future stretched out, a frightening unknown. Frightening, but for the thread of hope within, not only because of the optimism of youth, but also from her steadfast trust in her Heavenly Father. . .the father who wouldn't let her down. Or hadn't until now.

Grimacing, she stared back into the mirror, only to freeze as her eyes caught the reflection of her sister, over her shoulder, staring into the mirror at her. The stunning features of the older sister darkened threateningly.

Flinching, Deena swung about. "Elizabeth. . .Beth, what are you doing here?"

Struggling for composure, Deena searched the room. "Lord, what does it mean? Beth can't be here. She's in America with her husband. . .isn't she?"

Even as fear nagged, Isaiah 41:10 flashed in her heart. "Fear thou not; for I am with thee: be not dismayed; for I am thy God. . . ."

one

Striding into the sitting room, Mr. Kyle Stern flung himself into a wingbacked chair. His long, athletic form settled heavily into the chair, which, though sturdy enough to bear his large frame, still seemed almost Lilliputian against his broad shoulders, his long muscular arms and legs.

Unbuttoning his well-fitted jacket, he sighed, stretching out his long legs, heedless of the spattering of dust on his riding breeches or the mud on boots that no longer bore the polished shine so sought after by the London beaus.

Sucking in a long, deep breath, he exhaled slowly as he lay his head back against the chair. The room was silent, too silent.

Everything was in its proper place, from the rust, velvet-covered couches to the walnut gateleg table in the corner with the old family Bible laid precisely in the center on a white embroidered cloth. A cradle sat empty in the corner.

Pain flickered across the usually strong, impassive face. The cradle. "Lord, it's been three years, why can't I forget? Helen is right, I need to get on with my life."

"Papa!" six-year-old Amy screamed with delight as she catapulted into her father's arms. "Mrs. Cairn said you'd come in."

"Were you a good young lady for Mrs. Cairn?" he asked as he tucked strands of her blond hair behind her ear. For a moment he stroked the soft hair, hair that reminded him sharply of Lizzy.

He half expected Lizzy's green eyes to accost him rather than his daughter's shining blue ones. "Oh, Papa, Mrs. Cairn is so. . .so *slow!* I need to run, run, run." She spread her arms in emphasis.

Stern bit back a smile at the innocent exasperation. Amy knew what she was about, the little minx. So like Lizzy. *No!* He jerked forward with a violence that nearly toppled Amy from his lap. No, not like Lizzy!

He would see Amy had more discipline, understood right from wrong. Mrs. Cairn, as nice as she might be, served only as a temporary nanny at best. He must find someone who would help him curb his daughter's wilder tendencies while providing her with love and care.

Stern shook his head. The child had not known her mother since she was three and even then Lizzy had never been much of a mother to the child. Helen told him Amy needed a mother. The man's face hardened. Maybe so, but a governess would have to do.

Flinging her arms about his neck, Amy clung to her father, her eyes wide with questions. "Papa," the girl's anxious question broke in on his dark thoughts, "are you mad at me?"

Hugging the child to him fiercely, Stern said, "No, little squirrel. Not at you. Papa was just thinking."

" 'Bout Mama?"

Stern stared down at Amy in her stained brown frock. "What ever makes you say such a thing?"

"You always look angry when you're thinkin' of Mama." She pointed to the picture over the mantel.

In bewilderment, Stern glanced at the large picture an itinerant painter had done of his Three Oaks estate with its large, plantation-style house.

"Not here, Papa. The picture of Mama in the drawing room. You always frown when you see it." Her face showed puzzlement.

Stern sucked in a breath. Somehow he must keep his feelings more carefully hidden. Amy must not know about her mother, about Lizzy. "It's not important, little squirrel," he said, tickling her.

From far away, a bell sounded. Amy tensed. "Is Mrs. Billings comin' over again, Papa?"

Stern felt her tenseness. "Why no, Amy. Helen's visiting her sister in Boston for several weeks. You knew that."

Amy slumped against him. "Good! I want it to be just you and me."

Stern looked at his daughter in surprise. "I thought you and Mrs. Billings got along famously."

Amy squirmed. "Sometimes she's nice, but other times I don't like her much, Papa."

"You know Jesus wants us to love everyone."

"I know." Tears gathered in the little girl's eyes. "Please don't be angry with me."

Stern hugged his daughter to him. "Squirrel. I love you, and I'm not angry at you. But do try to get along with Mrs. Billings—she cares about us." He spoke with a gentleness that would have astonished most of his acquaintances.

A large manservant entered the family sitting room. At the sound of footsteps, all expression fled from Stern's face. "What is it, Bailey?"

Bailey thrust out his large square jaw. "Pardon, Mr. Stern, but you have visitors." He paused. "They have momentarily arrived in New Hampshire from England, sir."

Lifting Amy to the floor, Stern got to his feet. "Show them in, Bailey."

Bailey flung open the door. "Mr. Stern, may I present to you Miss Margaret Hastings and Lady Deena Heyford, Suffolk, England."

Heyford! The name crashed in on him like a blow. A deep frown creased his set mouth as he waited silently for the two ladies to approach him.

Ladies? No! He took in the elfin form and open innocent face of the smaller one. That hair! He surveyed it with undisguised astonishment. Could any natural hair be that fantasy shade of silver blond, especially on a young woman scarce more than a child? Her large gray eyes stared up at him apprehensively. His gaze shifted reluctantly to the older of the two, the girl's companion, no doubt.

"Mr. Stern?" At the slight inclination of his head, she continued. "I am Miss Hastings. And this, as you know, is your sister-in-law, Lady Deena Heyford."

"Why should I know this?" inquired Stern.

The petite young miss glanced at her taller companion,

who seemed nonplused at the question. "Did you not receive. . ." Deena stumbled. "Or, rather, did not my sister Beth receive a letter from my father's solicitor, Orrin Worth?"

Stern stiffened, "Your sister, Lizzy, whom you call Beth—a nickname she hated, by the way—has been dead these three years past."

Deena gaped at him. Her knees buckled. Stern grabbed her arm to keep her from pitching forward. Her arm felt so fragile beneath his large hand, he feared her bones would crumble under his touch. Margaret helped her sit down.

With a grunt, Stern rang for Bailey. Not long thereafter, Deena drank deeply of a tall glass of cider.

"Are you all right now?" The girl winced at his sarcasm.

Though Deena nodded, she remained so pale that guilt washed over Stern.

"How. . .did. . .Beth. . .die?"

"Childbirth." Swallowing with difficulty, Stern spoke more harshly than intended. "You didn't know?"

Frowning, he sat down opposite the women, scarcely noticing Amy scrambling up beside him. Somehow he could not bear the look in the girl's eyes. "I wrote," he said in his own defense.

"We received no such letter," whispered Deena. "Did you not receive the letter about me from Mr. Worth?"

"I did not."

Staring at him helplessly, Deena bit her lip. "It's just, just. . ." He watched her struggled with her tears. "Papa's dead."

Stern's frown deepened. "You need not have brought such news in person." Lizzy would hardly have cared.

Margaret straightened her shoulders. "You do not know the whole of it, sir. Lady Heyford is now an orphan.

"My intended, Mr. Worth," Margaret flushed delicately, "posted a letter to this account to acquaint your. . .late wife of her responsibility toward her sister."

Stern eyebrows rose. "Lizzy's dead!"

Margaret remained adamant. "Then, the duty naturally falls to you, sir."

With an impatient hand, Stern rifled his hair. "I've no desire to provide for a young woman scarce more than a child." His eyes darkened to a stormy gray, then softened somewhat as Deena shivered and clenched her gloved hands.

Her gaze shifted to Amy, who stared back curiously. "You my aunt? Aunt Deena? My *real* aunt. . .not like Mrs. Billings. She makes me call her Aunt Helen, but she's not really my aunt."

"How old are you, Amy?" Deena asked in her low, musical voice that fell kindly on Stern's ear.

"Six," Amy held up her fingers. "I am very big for my age. Papa says so," she boasted.

There was no disguising the softness in his face as he spoke to her. "That's right, Amy. You are very big for your age. Too big," he added dryly, "to play hide-and-seek with old Mrs. Cairn."

Her long eyelashes fluttered shyly as she smiled at Deena. "You could play with me."

"That is quite enough!" remonstrated her father, hating that manipulative gesture that reminded him so of Lizzy. Downcast, Amy returned to his side, but not before both she and Stern recognized the light of understanding in the eyes of her aunt.

"See, Papa. Aunt Deena would not mind," the girl crowed.

Deena's smile faded under Stern's cold, impaling gaze. "Amy. Run along upstairs. I must speak with. . .your aunt alone."

Recognizing the firm tone, Amy sighed. Dropping a quick curtsy to Deena and Margaret, she scooted from the room. Stern watched her go before turning his gaze back to Deena. "Surely there are relatives in England to which you can go."

"Lady Heyford has an uncle, the heir to the title, in fact," said Margaret.

Again Stern frowned, his face cold, hard. "Then, pray tell, why come all this way? Surely he's your guardian, Miss Heyford."

Deena stared at the floor.

"Well, why did you not stay with him?" Though he had no desire to feel anything for Lady Heyford, Stern sensed her pain, her struggle for composure.

As he again posed the question, his breath caught as she whispered, "He did not want me."

Not sure he heard correctly, Stern glanced at Margaret for confirmation. Margaret raised her chin defensively. "Mr. Stern, you need not concern yourself further. Mr. Worth and I are quite prepared to take in Lady Heyford. Lady Heyford will return to England with me."

"Margaret, you can't!" Deena protested. "There is no mon. . ." She stuttered to a halt.

Mr. Stern watched the color come and go from Deena's pale cheeks. "Am I to understand there is nothing left of the estate?" The last thing he wanted was to be guardian to a young miss who would serve as a constant reminder of Lizzy.

He saw Deena's discouraged slump, the single tear dropping onto her tightly clenched, gloved hands. Mayhap he was being unnecessarily harsh.

Another thought hit him. "Have you ladies had dinner?"

Deena did not answer. Only her hands showed how hard she was trying to hang on to her self-control. Stern admired that. Lizzy had never been one to hold in her feelings. Margaret answered for them both. "I'm afraid not, Mr. Stern."

"Then by all means, let me send Bailey to the kitchens. I am certain the cook can find something for you."

Margaret nodded. "That is most kind, Mr. Stern, but could we retire for the night and partake in our chambers? Lady Heyford has gone quite beyond the limit of her resources. The voyage was most distressing for her."

"As you wish, Miss Hastings." Getting up, Stern went to the bell cord to summon Bailey.

"Bailey, our guests shall be staying the night."

Bailey quirked an eyebrow. "Rooms have been prepared."

"See that a tray is sent up to them."

Margaret rose gracefully to her feet, but Deena struggled to rise, wincing as she shifted her weight onto her right leg.

Surprising himself as much as Deena, Mr. Stern held out his hands. "Let me assist you, Miss Heyford."

Gingerly, she put out her hands, her face mirroring her confusion at his unexpected gentleness as he raised her to her feet. Straightening quickly, she turned toward Margaret. With a cry of pain, she collapsed against him.

Her face aflame, she pushed away. "Please, forgive me." Before Stern could react, Deena burst into tears.

Reacting as he would to his own daughter in such a situation, Stern lifted the exhausted young woman into his strong arms. He liked the feel and softness of her and for a moment, just a moment, he felt himself soften toward her plight.

With Margaret following, Stern bore Deena up the stairs and down the hall behind Bailey, who flung open a door. "Lady Heyford's chamber. Miss Hastings, your room is next door."

Stern swung into the well-appointed bedchamber and set Deena on the edge of a rose-colored quilt that served as a coverlet to the lowpost bed with its ornately carved headboard.

Shyly glancing up at him, she stammered, "I am sorry I fell."

A slow smile spread across his usually stern face. "I believe," he said softly, "the apologies are mine. . .Deena." Without another word, he turned and left the room.

Back in his own bedchamber, Stern paced. *What am I going to do with the young miss?* He didn't like the feelings she brought out in him, didn't like feeling vulnerable. . .not again.

"Why, Lord," he muttered, "why this, just when I'm getting my life back together. I can't go through this again. I can't." Frowning, he stared out the window into the darkening sky. "She's not my responsibility, Lord. I'm sending her packing on the morrow."

All he heard was the whistle of the wind in the trees below.

two

The next morning, as Deena awoke, she slowly blinked her eyes in the bright sunlight flooding in from between the open, deep rose curtains at the windows. Not only had someone been in to open the curtains, but a new fire had been started in the fireplace across the room.

Smiling drowsily, Deena sat up, stretched. Gingerly, she rubbed her thigh, and moved the leg slowly. She breathed a thankful prayer as it obeyed her commands. That, more than all else, made her know she had slept long and well.

Stretching again before rising, Deena surveyed the room. Her eyes lit with anticipation as she saw the oak secretary with its case of book-filled shelves, but if Mr. Stern had his way, she'd never have the opportunity to read those books.

Soberly, she forced her eyes from the bookcase to the armoire and matching highboy. Glancing toward the hearth, her eyes moved to the cabriole-legged chairback settee before the fireplace.

Seeing a bell pull, she tugged on it. Not long thereafter, a stocky maid in a black bombazine dress, white apron, and mobcap answered her summons. She brought a pitcher of hot water with her, which she poured out for Deena.

As Deena washed up, she surreptitiously studied the other woman. The young woman, Deena surmised, was approximately Margaret's age. She wore a thin band on her left hand.

" 'Ow else may I help you, miss?" the maid asked, a pleasant smile on her face.

Deena smiled back. "I'd like to dress."

Nodding, the maid went to the armoire and opened the door. "What is your name?" asked Deena.

"The name be Esie Jane Crooks, Mrs. Crooks. They all call me Esie around here."

Deena smiled. "Been married long, Esie?"

"Five years." Esie drew a thin wool gown from the wardrobe. The blue gown had a deep V neckline and long leg-o'-mutton sleeves.

Deena talked to Esie while the maid helped her into the gown, tied the sash. "Have you any children?" Esie blushed as she held the soft silver slippers while Deena pushed her feet into them.

"Aye, a little gal, Nellie. Almost two now. Such a one fer gettin' into things."

Deena chuckled. Picking up the hairbrush, Esie began brushing the long silky locks. "Such lovely hair." She spoke with awe. "They say you be Mrs. Stern's sister."

"I am. I did not know she was. . .she was. . ." Deena could not yet bring herself to say the words.

Jesus, she prayed silently, *my family is gone. I didn't much like the idea of living with Elizabeth, but now there's no one, and I sense Mr. Stern doesn't much care for me. What am I going to do? What am I going to do?*

As though recognizing Deena's change of mood, Esie finished dressing Deena's hair in silence. Pulling the sides of the long hair up, Esie fastened it, letting the rest fall down Deena's back in a cascade of waves.

"There," Esie stepped back, surveying her effort with satisfaction, "you look right smart, miss." Then she muttered, "She ain't goin' ta like it, she ain't."

Deena glanced at Esie in the cheval mirror, wondering if she had heard correctly. "Esie. . ." She was about to question her when her door opened and Margaret walked in.

"Ah, good. You're up. I glanced in earlier but you were sound asleep."

Patting Deena's hair one last time. Esie put down the brush. "Thank you, Esie. That will be all for now."

Seeming surprised at Deena's gratitude, Esie nodded as she hurried from the room.

Deena turned to Margaret. "It felt good to sleep in. I do feel much better this morning."

Margaret smiled, "Morning! Deena, it's early afternoon."

"Don't jest, Margaret." Going to the window, Deena glanced up at the sun. "No wonder I feel so empty! How long have you been up—no, don't tell me. You've probably been astir since the dawn. Bet my dear brother-in-law is in a spin by this time."

Margaret sobered. "He wants to see us as soon as we've had luncheon."

As the large-boned housekeeper led them through the library, Deena slowed to take in the airy room with walls and furnishings all in an inviting shade of spring green, high ceiling, and shelf upon shelf filled with books. How different Three Oaks was from what she had envisioned, how different these shelves from the empty shelves of her home.

"Come along now," grunted Mrs. Bitley.

"Oh, please excuse me. Mrs. Bitley, isn't it?" The tight-lipped woman barely acknowledged Deena. Though she wanted more than anything to peruse the books, Deena followed the housekeeper who seemed, if possible, even more distant than Mr. Stern himself.

After a quick knock on the far door, Mrs. Bitley led them into a cozy, surprisingly sparse study. A large kidney-shaped desk dominated the room. Behind the desk, built around the large window was a large bookcase, also filled with books.

Scarcely could she take her eyes from them to survey the rest of the room, warm with rust-covered armchairs, curtains, and with a thick Turkish carpet under her feet.

Stern must be indeed deep in the pockets to afford the luxuries found in this lovely country estate. Nothing in these surroundings matched her rather bleak expectations of primitive conditions. Certainly, Deena thought, it outshone many an ancestral home of her homeland.

Hesitantly, she sat in the armchair facing the desk and the man who overpowered the room as much by a certain presence as by his physical size.

There was no mistaking the tenseness of her shoulders, the anxiety in her wide, questioning eyes.

"Lord, why do I care?" he breathed, glancing upward. During the long night, he had made up his mind to send them packing. *The chit could be no better than that coquette sister of hers. The family has done me enough hurt.*

Yet, his half-prepared speech seemed unnecessarily harsh in the presence of this young woman. "You shouldn't have brought her." His frustration turned on Margaret.

"Oooh!" Deena hugged herself.

Stern glanced at her in consternation. "Are you all right!"

"No, I'm not all right." Blinking back tears, Deena struggled to her feet. "I was foolish to think, even a moment, I might find a home here," she choked.

Her bottom lip trembled. "You're every bit as disagreeable as Beth! I'm sorry we bothered you, Mr. Stern. At least Margaret and Mr. Worth care enough to share what little they have with me."

"Deena," said Margaret faintly.

She appeared not to hear as she faced Stern, her body trembling, her eyes fearful. Stern moved his hands as though to ward off her accusations, only to have Deena flinch violently before him.

Shocked at her reaction, he placed his hands carefully down in front of him. "Please be seated. . .Deena," he said quietly. "Let's discuss this rationally." For a long moment, he stared at her pale face framed by that impossibly lovely hair. He wondered fleetingly what it would feel like, then shook his head. "Why did you assume I was going to hit you?"

Sitting back down, Deena glanced past him to the calf-covered volumes lining the bookshelves behind him. His eyes narrowed. "I want an answer, Miss Heyford. Who hit you?"

Pain flashed across her open face. "Beth," she whispered, blinking back tears. "Beth."

three

"I'm sorry, Mr. Stern," Margaret said, "but Lady Heyford has not pleasant memories of her sister. The truth of the matter is, Lady Deena did not wish to come under her sister's guardianship, Neither did. . ." Margaret snapped her mouth shut forbiddingly.

"Then the suggestion came from your fiancé, Miss Hastings?"

"La, Orrin insisted Beth had a moral, if not legal obligation to take in her sister." Bitterness tinged her words. "You see, Mr. Worth never knew Beth as did I."

Tenting his long fingers before him on the desk, Stern studied the slender woman whose prim self-control had begun to crack. "And just what have you against my late wife?"

Though she shifted uncomfortably, Margaret's lips stayed tightly closed. Deena shook her head.

"She won't tell you," Deena's face darkened with remembered pain, "but I will! Margaret's father was the Earl of Weshion. She and Beth grew up together."

Deena glanced over at Margaret with unmistakable compassion. "Margaret's father was an earl, much better, in Beth's eyes, than simply being the daughter of a baron.

"Beth and Margaret were planning their London season when," Deena paused, and Stern sensed she disliked putting her friend through these painful memories, "Margaret's parents were killed in a carriage accident, leaving Miss, actually Lady Hastings, on the eve of her season, without a pence to fly with. One would suppose her bosom friend Beth would have felt compassion for her, but no, Beth was delighted with the turn of events.

"At the time, my governess had given notice. Beth proposed to father that Margaret replace her. Father would not hear of it.

Instead, he asked her to come as my friend and companion.

"Truth to tell, we were both relieved when Beth went off to London and not long thereafter ran off with some wealthy American." Deena lowered her eyes.

"I see." Stern's eyes narrowed. "I'm sorry about your circumstance, but Lizzy was a product of English snobbery."

"Mayhap I should not feel so put upon now if your father, Miss Heyford," again he deliberately refused to use her title, "had deemed me of enough consequence to speak to me in person, however much he disapproved our union."

"Disapproved?" Deena stared. "We didn't even know what had transpired until Lizzy wrote months later telling us of this American with deep pockets whom she'd married."

"Is this true!" Stern leaned forward, his carefully schooled composure broken. "Are you telling me your father did not strictly forbid our marriage?"

Deena snorted. "He didn't even know Beth had a partiality for anyone, much less an unknown American! Later, Mama wrote Lizzy, but Lizzy wrote only one other time, to inform us of the birth of her daughter."

The two stared at each other. "Nothing more?"

"No," said Deena. "Mother was very hurt because she never knew what Beth was like, not really."

Stern slammed a fist on the desk, making Deena flinch. "I learned quickly enough what she was like!" At the fright in Deena's eyes, he controlled himself. *Lord, I can't turn her away, can I?*

With a trembling hand, he riffled his dark hair. "Until we sort this out, I'd like you to stay."

"I mislike putting off this decision," Margaret replied firmly. "I must sail in a fortnight."

"Surely we'll find a solution by then." Surveying Deena, Stern noticed that her gown, though of good material, was quite worn and threadbare. "What depleted the family coffers?" Sarcasm narrowed his eyes. "The usual, I suppose. The baize tables."

"Aye, Father gambled. Was wrong indeed of him." Squaring

her shoulders, she faced Stern.

Stern chuckled cynically even while admiring the young miss's courage in facing him. "Your erstwhile parent threw away his fortune on his own pleasures, common enough among members of the ton, I understand."

How often Lizzy had disparaged him by unfavorably comparing him to the fancy English lords who strutted about London. "Your English lords live their debauched lives eating, drinking, gambling and," he hesitated at the frown of disapproval in Margaret's face, "other nefarious activities." He bowed in Margaret's direction. "Those so-called 'gentlemen' have no compunction about neglecting their estates, their people, their wives, and children." His gaze lingered on Deena's worn gown.

Deena blinked back tears. "What right have you to judge Father, you who never knew him? You who cared not a whit the heartbreak you caused when you seduced my sister into running away with you without even attempting to contact the family."

Stern grimaced under her onslaught. So dear Lizzy had carefully orchestrated the whole thing, twisting him about her finger as though he were some besotted coxcomb, which indeed he had been.

"Papa did not gamble, not until after Mama died." Deena's voice shook. "After the death of first my mother, then brother in the war with Napoleon, he seemed to lose all reason for living. That's when he began to drink, to gamble heavily, and lose."

Stern surveyed the young girl who now slumped in her chair, the misery of her memories etched on her face.

"I'm sorry." He spoke with a quiet gentleness that almost reduced Deena to tears. "For now, at any rate, shall we call a truce?" Silently Deena nodded.

❧

Deena breathed in the fresh spring air as she surveyed the lawns sloping gently down from the front and sides of the house to a lovely garden. "Thank you, Lord, for bringing me here, even if only for a short time."

Carefully, Deena stepped on the mosaic rock walkway so as not to accidentally catch her toe on the edge of the stone.

"Auntie Deena! Wait up!"

Amy, her face wreathed in a large smile, tugged on the dark green cape hastily thrown over her light green muslin gown, the very embodiment of spring. Shyly, Amy slipped her tiny hand in Deena's as she glanced up into her aunt's face. "Come, Auntie Deena."

Again and again Amy stopped to share with her new aunt a special flower or bush, a special bench on which to sit, point out a squawking bird, a nest, until finally they ducked through the opening of Amy's very special secret, a hideaway behind a huge lilac bush guarding an opening to the walled-in rose garden.

Amy put both hands over her mouth to hold in her excitement as Deena gasped at the beauty of the garden just coming to life after a hard winter. Roses lined carefully tended walkways, circled and draped over branches of majestic oak and fir. Some smaller bushes were shaped into alcoves for statues. In the very center of the garden a dolphin fountain hissed gently into the air.

"This is beautiful!" Deena exclaimed. "Are you sure you're supposed to be in here?"

Amy avoided the question. "I never brought no one here, afore," she whispered. "Sure not an 'dult. Are you 'dult? You're like Papa. He is 'dult, but he is fun too. When she's not 'round."

Laughing, Deena hugged the little girl.

In the days that followed, she spent a great deal of time with Amy. It was as though they had a special need of each other—Amy for a mother figure to love her unconditionally, and Deena for untrammeled acceptance.

As days passed, Margaret's patience grew thin. "Does Mr. Stern intend on trapping me in this wilderness?" she asked Deena, "or is he setting us up only to throw us out at the last moment?"

As for Stern, he absented himself most of the time, coming

in late, often missing luncheon altogether. "Sorry," he explained tersely, "but this is a busy time."

One afternoon when Deena and Amy were in the rose garden, Stern's large shadow fell over them. Deena chilled under his penetrating gaze. Then Amy leaped into his arms and his face softened as his arms enfolded his daughter.

For a short while, he played with her before sitting down beside Deena on a marble bench under the shade of an ancient oak tree. Giving Amy a final hug, he sent her on her way. "Run along, little squirrel, Mrs. Cairns has a surprise for you in the kitchen."

Laughing, Amy bounced away down the path and disappeared through her secret entrance.

Swallowing, Deena straightened the skirt of her worn gown stained from her play with Amy.

"I suppose you wonder what I have decided."

"I do." Deena wished her voice didn't sound so hesitant. Something about Stern always made her feel unsure of herself. "Margaret's been working herself into a state over this delay. She's anxious to return to marry Mr. Worth."

"And you, Deena," Stern said with a gentleness which quickened Deena's heartbeat. "Do you also wish to return to England?"

Deena considered before answering. "I have nothing left in England. No home, no family. Margaret and Orrin would take me in, but," her face twisted with concern, "I don't feel right about adding to their financial burden or about being a third at their wedding. But. . .you don't want me to stay." Deena stared down at the toes of her shoes.

"You're good with Amy?"

"Of course," Deena's head shot up, "I love Amy. She's a delightful child—loving. warm, intelligent. She has a very sharp mind, you know. I've started teaching her to read from the Bible. . .you don't mind?"

"Of course not. Truth is, Amy needs someone young enough to play with her, yet old enough and educated enough to teach her."

Eagerly Deena leaned forward. "I would be honored to teach Amy, if you would allow me, Mr. Stern."

"Do you think you're old enough for the task?" As she turned her sparkling wide eyes on him, Stern cleared his throat as though he'd forgotten something, then continued, "There's no doubt of your intelligence, nor the sincerity of your feelings for my daughter."

"Of course, I'm old enough," laughed Deena. Much later, she wished she'd told him her age, but in the sunlit garden it didn't seem important.

They continued the conversation later in the library, with Margaret present.

"Your lawyer, Mr. Worth, is correct, of course. It is my Christian duty to take you in." He paused, then continued, "Amy will be excited about having her real live aunt as her new governess." When Deena paled, he added quickly, too quickly, "However, you'll be treated as one of the family." Without another word, Stern strode from the room, leaving the two young women staring at each other in surprise.

"Can this truly be God's will?" asked Deena tremulously.

"I don't know," said Margaret, squeezing her hand, "but I know God will take care of you wherever you are." Deena nodded, unable to speak around the lump in her throat.

Stern's nonchalant manner filled Deena with frustration. "You'll be Amy's governess," she mimicked the next afternoon as she sat alone on the garden bench. "Oh, and, by the way, you'll be treated as part of the family."

Blinking back tears, Deena slammed her fist on the hard marble, then groaned as it connected. She *was* family! She *was!* Miserably, she nursed her sore hand.

You are part of my *family,* came a quiet voice inside. *You belong to Me.*

Deena bowed her head. "I know, Lord. Thank You for reminding me, but I wish. . .oh I wish. . .to belong to someone here."

Leaving the bench, Deena headed toward the long, vine-covered stables. Inside the high arched walkway between the box stalls, she breathed in the fragrance of fresh hay, oats, liniment, ammonia, and other tangy horse odors.

The head groom, a lean man with thin hips, whose only concession to his advancing age was his thinning gray hair, nodded toward the sweet-faced young woman whose visits he had come to expect. "Cum ta see Princess, did you?"

"Yes, Jed," Deena said, before continuing down the long vaulted hall with rows of stalls on either side. For a moment she halted as her leg threatened to buckle. "Lord, please. Not now. Not here."

Another groom at his side, whom she recognized as Esie's cheerful husband, came up behind her. "You all right, miss?"

Rubbing her thigh, she gingerly stepped forward. The leg held. "Yes. Thank you, Crooks. I'll be fine now." Deena swallowed the embarrassment she invariably felt whenever her leg gave way on her.

A long black nose reaching over the open top of a stall distracted her. In a few strides, Deena reached the sleek mare. The dark horse shoved the white snip on her nose into Deena's chest, almost upsetting her.

"Whoa, girl," she laughed, patting the silky forelock hanging over the soft liquid eyes gazing out at her. Picking up a soft brush, Deena unlatched the stall door and slipped inside. Brush in hand, Deena began grooming the lovely, if sometimes skittish, mare.

Letting out a slobbery sigh, Princess relaxed under the gentle ministrations. Deena smiled dreamily, the rhythmic strokes helping calm her own chaotic emotions.

She wanted to stay with Amy, and she wanted to stay at Three Oaks despite the confusing behavior of its owner. She well knew he had decided she could stay for the sake of his daughter, whom he loved dearly. That was a high point in his favor. Deena sighed. From the way he prayed, she was certain he had a genuine relationship with God, but. . . .

Again she sighed. If she was to make Three Oaks her home, she would need be careful not to antagonize Mr. Stern. However did her volatile sister put up with her moody husband? Mayhap not well. It did not sound as though the marriage had been very happy.

With a last pat to the lovely mare, Deena let herself out of the stall. How fortunate she had discovered the neglected little mare. Just being with the horse calmed her frayed nerves. Old Jed had been delighted when she had given Princess the extra love and care the scarred and scared mare needed to once more trust humankind.

As Deena put away the brush and turned down the long hall, she prayed Stern would allow her to ride the fine horses stabled here, mayhap even Princess. At the thought, a smile crossed her lips.

Margaret met her inside the house. "Lady Heyford, Deena. Mr. Stern says we're leaving at dawn tomorrow for Portsmouth. He's sending me back to Orrin on one of his own ships, special passenger and all. I can hardly take it in."

Deena interrupted impatiently. "But you said I was to go?"

"I know. I don't understand it all except he has accepted full responsibility for you. He'll take care of you. Deena. He may be moody at times, but I believe him to be a good man. Says we are going to stay with his sister and her family in Portsmouth until everything is arranged."

Gulping, Deena forced herself not to reveal the turmoil she felt inside. Whatever else happened, she would not give her friend cause to worry.

four

Deena leaned back against the soft squabs of the traveling landau. The early morning breeze was nippy, and she was thankful the top was up and fastened.

Her attention moved from Margaret, who was keeping Amy enthralled with stories of her childhood in England, to the passing scenery out the open window. Dressed in a deep blue riding jacket, white breeches, and polished black riding boots, Stern rode alongside on an immense gray stallion.

The very sight of his commanding presence on the huge animal made Deena a trifle breathless. Disconcerted at her reaction. she jerked her eyes from the tall rider.

Midafternoon they arrived at a comfortable three-story red-brick-faced structure on a fashionable street in town. Deena shrugged. However fashionable the house, Deena's position was but that of a lowly relation no one truly wanted, a position lower than the one Margaret had enjoyed in the baron's home.

As soon as the landau stopped, Stern opened the door. Squealing, Amy leaped into his arms. Setting her on the walkway, he watched her dash up the steps to the heavy door held open by a hefty black butler.

"Hey, Saul," the little girl called cheerily.

Stern turned back to assist the ladies, helping first Margaret than Deena from the carriage. Carefully, he steadied Deena before releasing her, obviously recalling the embarrassing episode when first they met.

Offering each an arm, he conducted them regally to the door. Having never seen a man of color before, Deena tried not to stare at the black butler. Supposing he was a slave, she swallowed her outrage.

When Saul bounced the laughing girl on his shoulder, shock

reflected on Deena's face. Leaning down, Stern commented dryly. "Actually, we keep him shackled in the dungeon at night."

Deena turned toward him with wide, questioning eyes. A slight smile cracked across Stern's stern lips.

"Stop it, Kyle!" commanded a large buxom woman whose booming voice rippled with laughter.

"Saul, take Amy upstairs to play with Doris and Susan. Thank you," she said as he readily complied.

"Rhonda." Stern found himself enveloped in her ample arms. Deena grinned at the pained grimace on his face as he hastily disentangled himself with as much decorum as he could muster.

"Rhonda, I wish to make you known to Miss Heyford and her companion, Miss Hastings."

"Deena, Margaret, may I acquaint you with my sister, Mrs. Bates."

Mrs. Bates's eyes widened as she acknowledged the introductions. Her eyes mirrored questions as she glanced from Deena to her brother. He explained tersely. "Seems Miss Heyford is my ward, Sis." Deena blushed, for his tone gave little doubt what he thought of the arrangement.

"Fancy you a guardian, Kyle. Well, well. Come on in and sit down." She led the way to a cozy drawing room done in an assortment of colors and classic furnishings. The furniture appeared large and comfortable. Small statuettes and knick-knacks overflowed the side tables. The cozy warmth of the room reached out to enfold Deena.

"Now, dear," Mrs. Bates addressed Deena, "what brings you to New Hampshire?"

"My. . .my father died. His solicitor, lawyer, sent me to stay with Beth. There wasn't anyone else."

Mrs. Bates quirked a large eyebrow at her brother. "Beth?"

"Lizzy, of course," said Stern. "Seems the new baron refused to accept his responsibility and return from India. Correct?" He looked over at Deena.

Deena replied a bit too smartly for politeness, "Yes, sir.'"

If Stern's sister felt the constraint between the two, she gave no indication. " 'Tis a shame about Lizzy." Deena sensed the woman felt little regret. "Of course, Kyle will do right by you, Deena."

"Be company for Amy." His glance toward Deena made her clench her fists.

Lord Jesus, must he continually rub in the fact that this was the sole reason he agreed to take me in?

"Well, the child needs someone to attend her other than interfering neighbors."

Deena heard Rhonda's disapproval and wondered to whom she referred. "Does she know of this addition to your household?" Rhonda inquired.

Stern shook his head, "Been visiting in Boston. I'm sure she'll enjoy having another female to talk to. We're pretty isolated, you recall. Besides," he frowned, " 'tis my business . . .not hers."

"Umph!" His sister muttered. "That's one female who's not interested—" Deena missed the rest for at that moment, the door opened, admitting a tall slender man with sandy hair.

A welcoming smile spread across his thin face at the sight of his guests. After pecking his wife's ample cheek and firmly shaking hands with Stern, he smiled toward the two young ladies. "And who are these charmers, Kyle?"

Almost reluctantly, or so it seemed to Deena, Stern introduced them. Whatever reservations she might have had about Stern's family were swept away by the man's hearty welcome.

"Good for you, old chap!" James Bates slapped Kyle on the shoulder when informed of the guardianship. Stern grimaced.

Deena was relieved when a lovely maid, about her own age, summoned them to luncheon. Deena had the oddest impression the maid was not what she seemed to be, but dismissed the thought as foolishness.

The informality about the table caused Deena to further withdraw. Across the table she caught Stern's gaze and was surprised by the rueful, if silent, sympathy expressed in his dark eyes.

"Now this afternoon. . ." Rhonda chatted on, obviously enjoying organizing the lives of those in her sphere of influence. Deena suppressed a giggle.

"Rhonda," Stern interrupted his sister midsentence, "I'm taking Deena downtown. Her wardrobe is a disgrace. I'm certain Miss Hastings will assist me in choosing an appropriate wardrobe for my ward."

Fork halfway to her lips, Deena froze. Color drained from her cheeks, leaving her even paler than usual. She ducked her head in embarrassment under his assessing gray eyes.

A brief smile touched his lips as he watched her reaction, but suddenly she raised her head and stared at him, her mouth set, her eyes flashing. With a nod of approval he turned away, leaving Deena bewildered.

After luncheon, the coachman drove the landau downtown to the shops catering to the fastidious men and women of means and stopped in front of a shop with large front windows where velvet curtains lifted to reveal the latest in chic fashion from Paris.

Seeing Margaret's longing gaze at the window, Deena whispered. "Please, Mr. Stern, I don't need much. Would I be too bold to ask if you would buy Margaret a gown instead?"

Stern stared at her with incredulous disbelief. Deena bit her lips. "She hasn't had a new gown in ever so long."

Respect flashed in Stern's eyes before his usual mask of mistrust descended. Effortlessly, he swung her down beside her companion. Holding out his arms, he escorted the ladies into the shop. His presence immediately commanded the attendance of the modiste. "Mr. Stern, how may I serve you?"

Stern answered for them. "Lady Heyford has become my ward, Mrs. Bell. It is essential she have the clothes proper to her station." Deena bit back a grin at his use of the title.

The dressmaker was suitably impressed. "Of course, Mr. Stern. We shall serve you as always." Consternation crossed her face as Stern's frown deepened. Margaret and Deena exchanged a puzzled glance at the unexpected tenseness between the dressmaker and Stern.

Stern spoke first. "As to Lady Hastings. . .see she, too, is provided several new gowns. One is to be a white silk evening gown." A genuine smile touched his lips at the astonishment on the faces of the two younger women.

A white gown! Of course! Deena turned eager eyes toward her friend.

Margaret shook her head. "Mr. Stern, I could not, really. . ."

"Think of it as Lady Heyford's wedding gift to you. I dare say you have not been compensated for some time." At Margaret's telltale blush, he nodded. "Then consider this what is due." He turned once more to the dressmaker, who was already calculating her profits.

"You will, of course, provide all the essentials and fripperies to go with the gowns." With that startling statement, he found himself a padded arm chair against the wall. Before seating himself, he impaled the dressmaker in his intimidating gaze. "Bell, I wish to see whatever gowns I purchase for my ward. Umm, I might add, they shall be appropriate to her youth and station."

The dressmaker's eyelids flickered momentarily. Watching her face, Deena was certain Stern conveyed a message beyond her own ken to comprehend.

Sometime later, Deena gingerly followed the modiste out to where Stern waited, legs crossed, idly glancing about the long room crowded with bolts of cloth, chairs, dummys wearing the latest Parisian style, and a few elegantly gowned customers speaking together in hushed tones as they waited.

At the woman's command, Deena shyly showed off her gown for her guardian. Finally Stern nodded. "We'll take it." Deena sighed. The dressmaker glowed.

The afternoon proved long and tiring as Deena modeled one gown after another to her critical guardian, who was not above suggesting changes or dismissing a gown or pattern.

"Too much décolletage. She's not to appear like some hussy. Color, all wrong. No pastels. Washes her out. Lady Heyford needs bright colors. She's already too pale by half."

After a long while an exhausted Deena scarcely noticed the

cut or fit of the gowns she modeled until the pink. "I don't think," she began, troubled by the expanse of skin showing.

Bell paid her no mind. "Come along now, Lady Heyford."

Reluctantly, Deena modeled the gauze gown, which sensuously draped her slender figure. She was not prepared for Stern's violent reaction.

His eyes glazed angrily as he clutched the arms of the chair. Deena froze. Even the modiste retreated from his fury. "Mr. Stern, I—"

"Take that gown off this instant, Deena." He leaned toward her as though to grab her. Tears sparkled in her tired eyes. "I will do so, Mr. Stern. Truly, I do not like it. Please!"

Her distress communicated itself to Stern and his face softened, then hardened again as he glared at the dressmaker. "I gave you explicit instructions as to what I consider suitable for Lady Heyford. If these are not strictly adhered to, I shall take my ward and my purse elsewhere."

Hurrying Deena from the room without a word, Bell all but ripped the gown from her. She made no other mistake. Then came that one special gown that made Deena gasp.

"Mr. Stern, Lady Heyford," Bell motioned for Deena to turn slowly to show off the pale satin gown that floated about her white shoulders in a delicate touch of confection and lace. The bodice molded her slim, maturing figure to the tight waist. The skirt swirled out from Deena's tiny waist in a kaleidoscope of silver and white from the silver threads shot through the material. The sleeves puffed at the shoulders, then fit tightly to the wrists with a row of pearl buttons.

Excited about showing off the gown, Deena turned more sharply than intended. Her leg twisted, buckled. Stifling a cry, Deena fell. In one smooth motion, Deena felt arms grabbing her. A moment later her heartbeat marched with that of her guardian, as he held her tightly to his chest. Only much later did she recall how fast his heart beat under her ear.

Grasping her shoulders, Stern steadied her. Then with a smile, he said, "We'll take the gown." Reluctantly, Stern released Deena.

"Bell, if Miss Hastings has her things selected, I suggest we finish up here."

Stern even smiled as he lifted Deena into the waiting landau, assisted the grateful Margaret, and swung in opposite them. "I hope you're satisfied with your purchases, Miss Hastings," he commented with only a hint of sarcasm.

Margaret flushed like a schoolgirl under his scrutiny. "Mr. Stern, it was most generous of you."

Deena grinned. "Oh, Margaret! I had to force you to take that one gown." She turned to her guardian. "She was about to settle for this hideous gown of some rough yellowish white material instead of the one of white silk."

As she animatedly began describing the gown, Margaret hushed her. " 'Twould have done right well for me, milady."

"Phooey! Must be addlepated to prefer that horrible thing to the smashing silk."

" 'Twas so expensive," Margaret murmured, her eyes on Stern apologetically.

He glanced at Deena sharply. "She spoke for the silk?"

"I insisted!" Her eyes flashed defensively. "You did say was to be my gift." Her voice wavered uncertainly. "Your pockets aren't to let, are they?"

"Lady Heyford, your manners!" Margaret reprimanded.

"I just meant. . .I mean. . .not like Father after Mother died. . ."

The pleasant expression on Stern's face hardened into his usual cold, cynical mask. "Never fear, Miss Heyford, I am sufficiently wealthy. I'm not given to gaming away *my* inheritance. I would not do it for Lizzy and I won't do it for anyone else, either."

Deena colored and stared unseeing out the window as she fought conflicting emotions of hurt, humiliation, and confusion. Sighing, she gave up trying to understand how she felt. *Lord, I don't understand why he unsettles me so.*

Clattering down the cobblestone streets to the wharf, the landau stopped. "Wait here," Stern instructed, climbing from the carriage. Moments later, he disappeared among the many squat square buildings surrounding the quay.

After a questioning look, Deena and Margaret watched the sailors bustling about, lifting barrels and boxes. They smelt the brine of saltwater, caught the familiar scent of tar and cordage. Deena flinched at the language exchanged by the sailors and other workers at top volume down the pier.

Margaret murmured impatiently, "What's keeping him?"

"Here he comes." Shading her eyes, Deena watched him striding toward them, heads and shoulders above the heavily muscled seamen who made way for him as though he were some royal personage. Gladness filled her at the sight of him, sweeping away her confusion.

As he took his place once more in the carriage, she smiled at him. Uncomfortable, Stern cleared his throat. "My apologies for keeping you ladies waiting. Miss Hastings, I have spoken with my nephew who captains my ship, *The Elizabeth*. The ship is already loaded and ready to depart for England. You shall be aboard. You shall be safe under the protection of Jonathan Edwards. At Southampton he'll see to a carriage to take you to your Mr. Worth." He paused. "I hope this meets with your approval, Miss Hastings."

Stunned, Margaret stared at him. Deena clapped her hands. "Margaret, how wonderful! Thank you, Mr. Stern!" She glanced at her guardian. "Jonathan Edwards? You have a nephew named after the preacher who brought the Great Awakening to the colonies? Any relation?"

Stern's eyebrows raised. "Jonathan comes by his name on the Bates side of the family." Taken back by the gleam of interest in her eyes, he studied the young woman across from him. "The family were communicants of his congregation in Northampton, where Edwards ministered for over twenty years." He expected her interest to fade.

"I suppose after dismissing the great preacher, they suffered guilt that carried into the next generation."

She jolted him with her intimate knowledge of the situation. "Not quite," he drawled, though his eyes watched Deena's face intently. "Thoroughly in agreement with Edwards's views, the family was shaken by what happened. Edwards himself helped Bates's uncle enter seminary.

"He became a well-known evangelist in the western territories. Charged the whole clan with fervency. My nephew's brother Daniel has entered the seminary." He smiled slowly, his eyes lidded but watchful. "I'm not quite the prodigal you would have me be."

Flustered, Deena lowered her eyelashes.

As Rhonda exclaimed over the light muslin gown Deena had worn back from the shop, Amy ran up to her father.

"Papa, did you buy lots and lots for Auntie Deena? You know," she said seriously, "her clothes are very old."

Deena blushed, but Stern only laughed as he picked up his daughter and hugged her before putting her down again. Her two cousins, Doris and Susan, stared up at their uncle out of wide brown eyes. "Why don't you girls help Saul carry the packages up to Miss Heyford's room?"

"Careful with them, girls," Rhonda called after them as they scrambled to intercept Saul and another servant in the hall.

Stern noted Deena's questioning glance as the black man handed each little girl a small package. Once in the sitting room, he said, "Saul is free, Miss Heyford."

"Oh, I didn't know. I am sorry."

Stern addressed his sister. "With me as an example, there has been little reason for our English rose to think of us as anything but savages, right, Deena?" He chuckled.

Rhonda broke the uncomfortable silence. "A business acquaintance of the family has recently returned from England. James has invited him for dinner." She threw a look of warning toward her brother. "I expect everyone to be on their best behavior."

five

Margaret smiled at Deena, who returned it with a grin. "Don't we look comely! Why, Margaret, you look wonderful in that gold and green silk! Orrin will pop his quizzing glass."

Margaret laughed. Her eyes sparkled as she smoothed out an imaginary wrinkle in the lovely gown. "What about you?"

Turning slowly before the cheval mirror, Deena viewed her white velvet dress. Fine red ribbons and lace marched down the full sleeves. A matching wide sash emphasized her exquisite waist. "Mr. Stern went all out for us, didn't he?"

The maid attending them gave Deena's hair a last pat after fastening it back with long red lace ribbons. "There you are, Miss Heyford."

"What's your name?" Deena asked the maid whose fine features drew her curiosity.

"Andrea, miss. Is there anything else?"

"No. Thank you." Thoughtfully, Deena watched the young woman gracefully exit the chamber.

Margaret heard her sigh. "Are you all right?"

"Guess I am a bit tired, nothing serious." She smiled.

"Your leg?"

"Sore." Absently, she rubbed her thigh. "I pray it doesn't give me any trouble tonight."

"Have you told Mr. Stern about your problem?"

Deena shook her head. Margaret frowned. "Promise me you'll tell him soon." At the obstinate look in Deena's eyes, Margaret's face hardened. "Promise, or—or I won't go down to dinner."

"That's blackmail! Of course you must go to dinner. Why, you must let them see your new gown! No one will look at anyone but you."

"Now promise, Lady Heyford."

"Oh, all right. I'll tell him. Soon," she added at Margaret's insistence.

In comfortable companionship, the two young women entered the parlor. Glancing up from his conversation with James, Mr. Stern surveyed Margaret's attire with an approval that brought a healthy color to her cheeks. Seeing Deena beside her, his eyes widened in admiration.

She curtsied. "Do I meet with your approval, sir?"

"You do me proud, Deena," he said, his voice unusually deep and solemn. His eyes strayed again and again to the cascade of hair sparkling in the candlelight.

"Why, don't you two look lovely," Rhonda boomed.

"Mrs. Bates."

"Rhonda. We're not formal around here, my dear." She nodded her satisfaction at the gowns. "Kyle always did have excellent taste, not like some I could mention."

The reference was lost on Deena, who bit back a giggle. Rhonda herself was outrageously gowned in satin lavishly embroidered with large wildflowers. A large diamond necklace dangled from her neck, matching heavy jewelry weighted down her ears and arms.

Rather too loudly, she whispered, "It's quite all right, dear. James likes me in it." Then she winked.

Even as Deena relaxed, a familiar, arrogant voice cut through Deena's growing security like a deadly knife. "Rhonda, James. Good to see you again, Kyle." Clyde Porter turned slowly, his feral eyes devouring Deena.

She froze as he came toward her, a mocking smile on his face. "Lady Heyford. Deena! Fancy meeting you here." Reluctantly, she permitted him to take her cold hands, then shuddered inwardly as he lifted one then the other to his lips.

Stern's face darkened. Deena tugged her hands from Clyde's possessive grasp. "Miss Heyford," he said as she shrank from his biting sarcasm. "I was not aware you were so well acquainted with Mr. Porter."

"No. . .yes." Stumbling, Deena tried to explain.

"Don't get yourself in a spin, Kyle. The lovely lady and I

became very good *friends* on the trip over." Miserably, Deena blinked back tears at the inference, which brought a scowl to Stern's face.

Clearing her throat, Rhonda smiled and said, too brightly, "I had not realized you had met Kyle's ward, Clyde."

"Ward?" This startled him. "So you'll be making your home at Three Oaks." His laugh grated down Deena's spine. Had it been possible, she would have sworn her guardian's cold mask hid burning, barely suppressed fury.

"Surely, Kyle, you won't mind if I find my way down to Three Oaks." His eyes remained on Deena.

Did he think Stern would countenance his unwanted boorishly rude behavior? Then, of course, rightly speaking, Stern did not consider her part of the family, only an unpaid retainer. She heard tell how governesses were often considered fair game for the likes of men like Porter.

Deena blinked back her tears. Beside her, Margaret squeezed her hand reassuringly. Deena held on, desperately wishing Margaret was not leaving. Mayhap would be safer if she herself returned to England.

There was no going back, Deena knew that, not with all her new guardian had already done for her. . .and especially for Margaret. She would not take any chances with Margaret's happiness. After all, wouldn't the Lord protect her?

Pasting a weak smile on her face, Deena looked at her friend with what she hoped was reassurance.

At the dinner table, Deena merely pushed her food around her plate while eyeing Porter sitting far down the table. At her left her guardian regarded her with skepticism. She did notice he did no more justice to his meal than she did to hers.

As she got up from dinner to join Rhonda, she was surprised the men also rose to their feet to accompany them from the room. Deena wondered if it were an American custom for the gentlemen not to linger at the table drinking port and brandy or whether this was because both her guardian and the Bateses were teetotalers.

As Porter swerved her way, she tensed. As he reached to

take her arm, Stern stood beside her. "May I, Lady Heyford?" His eyes met those of Porter over Deena's head.

Porter's lips tightened. Bowing with a curt mockery Deena failed to understand, he turned to take Margaret's arm. Relieved, Deena flashed her guardian such a look of relief, his mask dropped momentarily. Returning her look with a questioning smile, he took her arm and followed his sister, leaning on the arm of her husband, down the wide wainscoted hallway.

"This way," Rhonda boomed. "Have a surprise in the music room."

A footman flung open the chased-paneled doors to a vaulted room with walls covered with flecked rose and silver silk. A rosewood spinet dominated the room on a special dais beneath Venetian crystal chandeliers.

Much to her relief, Stern seated Deena beside him on a graceful Sheraton settee facing the dais. Porter escorted Margaret to a nearby chair. At the sight of Stern comfortably ensconced beside Deena, his face darkened.

Momentarily, Porter's gaze locked with hers. Shuddering, Deena leaned closer to her guardian. Stern glanced at her in surprise, then, seeing her gaze, deliberately enfolded her hand in his own. Taking the hint, Porter sat elsewhere. When Stern released her hand, it tingled warmly and Deena felt a sense of loss.

Fit for Bedlam, she thought, *if a mere gesture sets me in a spin.* She sensed his gesture had something to do with Porter, though she didn't fully understand.

A squeal of delight brought her attention to the dais where three young girls smiled at the assembled family and guests. Amy looked adorable in her white satin gown with a bright yellow sash and matching hair ribbons.

Amy, the smallest and youngest of the three cousins, curtsied before sitting down at the spinet. Turning, she grinned toward Deena and her father before putting her hands on the keys. With her face set in an expression much like one Deena had seen on the face of her father, Amy played a simple melody. As the last note died away, Amy jumped from the dais and ran to her father as everyone applauded.

"How did I do, Papa? Did I surprise you? Auntie Deena taught me that song, didn't you, Auntie Deena?"

Deena smiled warmly. "I'm proud of you, Amy, very proud."

Stern hugged his daughter. "I'm proud of you too, little squirrel." When he would have pulled her into his lap, she retreated. "Not now, Papa. I have to help Doris and Sue." With a decided flounce that brought a frown to Stern's lips, Amy ran back to her cousins.

Proudly, the little girl leaned forward, ready to turn pages for Doris, who at the advanced age of nine prepared for her stint at the piano by massaging her long fingers. To the left, twelve-year-old Susan readied her violin. Moments later Deena closed her eyes, relaxing under the influence of the startlingly moving, if abbreviated, rendition of Beethoven's Fifth.

The musical concert continued for another hour. Proudly, Amy sang two numbers with her cousins accompanying her. More than once Deena glanced at her guardian, detecting a strange sadness in his eyes as he looked at his daughter.

Once he caught her gaze on him and returned it, devoid of emotion, until she looked away. What folly to think she read some caring behind that cold mask.

Unable to forestall it any longer, Deena yawned behind her gloved hand. Margaret noticed. "If you'll excuse us, I believe Lady Heyford and I shall retire. We are quite fatigued."

The girls, who had finished their concert and were indulging in a treat of hot chocolate and scones, glanced up. Susan, tall and gangly and showing the promise of womanhood, rolled her eyes at the other two girls. "Uh-oh!"

Chuckling, Rhonda gathered the three girls in an ample hug. "Time for you sweets to be abed."

Doris groaned. Eyeing her father, Amy continued eating. "Enough, Amy," he said sternly, "come say good night."

Reluctantly, the older girls said good night, then waited while their young cousin flung herself into the arms of her father. "Papa, do I hafta go to bed? Do I?"

"Yes, you 'hafta'," he repeated, laughing. "Now bid your aunt good night."

Releasing her father, Amy put her arms around her aunt. "I loves you, Auntie Deena. Nite."

"Good night, dear." Her heart ached for the motherless child.

As the girls ran off to bed, James suggested they move to the more comfortable family parlor. In the wake of the girls' departure, Margaret's declaration was forgotten. As the others walked on ahead, Deena edged toward the stairs and stumbled. A strong hand grabbed her in time to keep her from falling. Still shaking from her close call, Deena, eyes lowered, allowed her rescuer to escort her into a dimly lit sitting room.

All she needed to do was rest a moment until her trembling eased. Deena turned to thank her benefactor, only to stare up into the mocking face of none other than Clyde Porter!

"Nice piece of acting. How like Lizzy you are, my lady."

Deena flinched as though he had slapped her. "I thought you were. . ." she bit her lip.

Porter's eyes narrowed. "So that's your approach. Can't wait to get your sister's husband alone." He laughed hollowly. "From appearances, I'd guess he already sits in your pocket." He moved closer, his eyes on Deena's white face.

"You may have escaped my attentions about ship by staying in your room, but we're not aboard ship now. Lizzy may have danced me a fine tune before submitting to my caresses. I'll not take that off some unfledged chit."

Horror spread over Deena's face as his ominous words sunk into her benumbed mind. "Beth would not. She was married!" Even as she made her assertion, Deena gulped. "I am not playing some game. I am not Beth!"

Porter snickered. "Ah, no indeed. She was a much more cozy armful than you'll ever make."

Deena's eyes flashed. Her hand smashed stingingly against Porter's evil grin. Stiffening in anger, he grabbed her wrist, twisting it painfully behind her back until Deena cried out, his contorted face inches from her own. Afraid of falling, Deena struggled to stand upright but with each movement her arm twisted, and her leg threatened to give way.

"Have done, sir," she pleaded, trying to quell the fear swelling inside her.

Porter laughed. "I have a partiality for hair such as yours." He tangled his free hand in her hair, pulling it from its restraints.

Deena's struggles were to no avail as he held back her head. "Let me go, you blackguard."

Slowly he forced her head toward his. Despite the pain, Deena twisted away. Porter's eyes glistened angrily. "Don't dare do that again. . .or I'll make you sorry. You will not play games with me."

"No! No!" Tears choked Deena's throat, making her words thick and unnatural.

Neither heard the door open. Suddenly, like an avenging angel, Stern's visage, darkened with fury, appeared over Porter's shoulder.

"Better leave me alone, Porter. My guardian is here!"

Porter's mocking laugh haunted Deena. "You think me fool enough to fall for such an obvious ruse?" He twisted her arm until Deena groaned. "Your guardian is happily ensconced with his foolish sister."

"I think not, Clyde!"

Porter released Deena so quickly she crashed to the floor. He whirled to face Stern's fury, all the more frightening for his rigid self-control, all the more dangerous.

"Just having a bit of a coz with Lady Heyford." Unable to meet Stern's blazing eyes, his arrogance floundered.

"Get out, Clyde. Get out. I'll see you never again enter this house you hold in such derision. . .nor mine!"

Paling, Porter nonetheless shot back. "You could not keep me from warming Lizzy's bed. Do you think her little sister is any different?" He closed the door softly behind his retreating frame.

Stern stared down at Deena, who pushed herself to a sitting

position while rubbing the welt on her arm. "Let me see that!" Stern squatted beside her and took her arm gently. Deena flinched at his touch. "He hurt you."

"La. Thank you for the timely rescue." She trembled under Stern's suspicious gaze.

"You didn't come to the parlor, neither did Clyde." He snorted softly. "From what Clyde said earlier I suspected some kind of dalliance."

Blinking back tears, Deena pushed herself to her feet. "You have it all wrong."

"Do I now?" Suspicion lurked in Stern's dark eyes as he sat down beside her.

Miserably, she sunk into a nearby couch. "So you're assuming all sorts of sordid happenings. You're worse than the London gossips. He said awful things about Beth. They can't be true. Beth was wild, even mean, but he said she was no better than. . ." Her lips refused to form the word aloud.

"Will these do?" Stern's face twisted cynically. "Tease, light skirt, hussy. You obviously knew little of your sister's proclivities." A sadness touched his eyes. "Lizzy quickly grew bored of being the proper wife of a straitlaced country gentleman."

"I don't understand."

Stern sighed, a long, bitter sigh. "Better to know the truth from me." He stared at the far wall. "I didn't even know who fathered the child she last carried."

"Yours?" whispered Deena, wishing to cover her ears.

Stern snorted. "Not a chance. We hadn't been together for more than a year. You do understand what that means, do you not?"

Deena's chest tightened, tears stung her eyes. A nightmare. It had to be a nightmare. Clutching her hands, she fought for control.

As though unable to help himself, Stern reached for her hand. "Your hand is cold. Are you all right?"

Deena snatched it away, eyes wide and frightened.

Stern forced himself to a calmness he did not feel. Putting

his arm about her, he gently pulled her resistant body against the warmth of his chest. Part of him saw her as a helpless young innocent, yet suspicion lingered. Was she merely playing a part to engender his sympathy after being caught out? It was a game her sister knew well. The whole of it smelled. Even Clyde wouldn't accost a guest in the house of another without invitation. . .would he?

"Did he. . .hurt you?" Touching her bruised wrist lightly, he asked, "Besides this?"

Deena glanced up. "No, I. . .can't. Please."

Lifting her face to his, he commanded. "What happened?"

"My leg gave out on me." She paused, bit her lip. "Since my accident, it. . .it does that, especially when I'm tired."

"Why?"

"Some years ago a horse fell on me, mangling my leg."

"Tonight?"

"Someone grabbed me, kept me from falling. I thought. . ." Deena lowered her thick dark lashes to hide the confusion in her eyes. "I thought it was you. Since I needed to rest a moment, I permitted myself to be led into this room. But it wasn't you, it was *him*." Deena's whole body tensed with the horror of it.

Stern broke in, "You did know him, then. Clyde spoke the truth."

"Yes, he traveled on the same ship as we. I did all I could to avoid him, but, he caught me out. . .tried to. . ." She wiped an expressive hand across her mouth. "Toward the end I scarcely left my cabin. Margaret will attest to that." She grimaced. " 'Twas dreadful." She shivered. "He said dreadful things about Beth, said I was like her. I'm not like that. I'm not!"

Did she protest too much? wondered Stern. *Lord, what do I say? Is Deena an innocent and how can I know for sure?*

"I'd like to believe you, Deena, but—"

Tears trickled down Deena's face. "I should have known you wouldn't believe me," she whispered. "My sister must have hurt you dreadfully for you to hold me in such distrust."

Awkwardly, Stern put his arm about her, letting her cry.

Wonderingly, Stern stroked the hair that eddied about Deena's shaking shoulders like molten star shine.

He had no idea how long he held her against him, surrounding her with his warm comfort. The girl warmed a piece of his heart, hardened with past hurts and cynicism. If only he could be sure of her. If only he could be sure she was different from Lizzy.

Deena cried until all her tears were spent. Slowly she relaxed in the warmth and security of Stern's arms.

Finally Deena pushed herself away from her guardian. Instantly, Stern released her. Looking up, Deena beheld the smile of genuine concern on lips. With his thumb, he wiped a large tear from her cheek. "Feel better?"

"I think so," she whispered. Suddenly she noticed his damp linen shirt, the stained black satin evening jacket. "Oh, dear, I've ruined your clothes!"

With his hand he gathered her long hair off her shoulders. "There are more important things than clothes."

Deena smiled crookedly. "I've always misliked women who fainted or cried at the slightest provocation."

"You had more than enough provocation, my dear. Clyde ever was an ill-bred bounder, despite his high-flown airs. I suggest you stay away from him."

"I'll do my best." Deena shuddered. "He's an evil man."

"Quite," Stern agreed. He resisted the urge to stroke her hair once more. "I think it best we keep this incident to ourselves."

Deena's eyes widened at her disheveled appearance. "Yes, of course. I must go to my room at once."

"Come then, little one." Unfolding himself from the couch, he assisted Deena to her feet. Taking her arm, he led her surreptitiously up to her chamber. "Now, my dear, before I am discovered, let me bid you farewell." With a smile that warmed Deena's heart, Stern departed.

Staring after him, Deena wondered why her heartbeat quickened.

six

From the carriage, Deena and Amy once more waved toward the ship that was taking Deena's companion back to England, back to the arms of the man who loved her.

"Godspeed," Deena whispered, wiping sweaty palms on the skirt of her white gown with its bright green trim that matched the green ribbons trimming her chip straw hat. Faintly she smiled toward Amy, who wore a green ruffled dress of the same shade as her own.

Sensing Stern watching from half-closed eyes, Deena prayed he wouldn't notice her attempt to stem the tears stinging her eyes, the trembling of her chin.

Inside she had a cavernous empty feeling of abandonment. Gone, her last link with home.

"Deena, don't worry about Margaret, God will take care of her." Stern paused. "Ready to go home?"

Sucking in a deep breath, she met Stern's gaze. "Yes, I'm ready to go back to Three Oaks." She could not yet claim it as home. If Stern understood her hesitation, he gave no sign.

The rest of the trip went as pleasantly as a trip could over rough roads in a well-sprung coach. Deena, as much to distract her own depressing thoughts as to entertain her niece, told her Bible stories using vivid word pictures.

"Then there was Ruth," said Deena. "After the death of her husband, she left everything, home and family, to follow her mother-in-law back to Israel."

"Why did she do that?" asked the little girl.

"Because she'd come to believe in Naomi's God, our God." Deena continued. "When they needed food, Ruth went out to the fields and gathered grain after the harvesters."

"God wasn't doing a very good job of taking care of them, was He?" Amy's eyes flashed.

"Yes, yes, He did," cried Deena. "They just couldn't see it then. It's like a puzzle, while we just see a piece, God sees the whole puzzle all put together. Because she had to gather the grain, Ruth met a man who fell in love with her named Boaz. He was not only kind, but wealthy."

"And he married Ruth and took care of Ruth and Naomi. Right?"

"That's right. But God had one more special reward for them. Do you remember King David?"

The little girl nodded.

"Well, the son of Boaz and Ruth was King David's grandfather, and you know what else?"

Amy shook her head. "Their son became an ancestor of Jesus."

"Ohhh."

Every once in a while, Deena glanced up to meet Stern's penetrating gaze. "You're obviously well-read," he said. His slow smile warmed Deena all the way to her toes. "I'm glad you're teaching her about the Lord." Left unspoken was the implication that this was unlike Lizzy.

Deena wondered if she'd ever get out from the heavy shadow of her sister's misdeeds. She'd come to see that Stern didn't trust easily and once that trust was broken, was slow to trust again. On the other hand, his loyalty and trust in his friends was unstinting.

The open gates of Three Oaks beckoned invitingly and the large windows twinkled in the rays of the afternoon sun as though welcoming them home. Mrs. Bitley squelched the welcome as she grimly took Deena's green cape. Her shrewd eyes chilled Deena.

Stilling a shudder, Deena made her way up the stairs.

"Missy, you all right?" Esie's concern startled Deena.

"Nothing really. Just Mrs. Bitley. She looks at me as though she'd like to stick a dagger in my back."

Esie shrugged her wide shoulders. "No love fer you, that's sure." Esie began unpacking the trunks of new clothes already deposited in the room. Stern had sent another carriage back filled with the many items he had purchased not only for her, but also for himself and Amy in the few days they had spent in Portsmouth.

"Old Bitley knows she ain't gonna like havin' another woman about."

"Everyone keeps making veiled references. To whom are you referring?"

Deena felt Esie's compassionate gaze. "Some wemmin be like that. Cain't stand competition."

"Me! Competition! What nonsense! I'm only Mr. Stern's ward, reluctant one at that."

Since Deena saw herself in the role of glorified servant, she wondered whether or not Stern expected her to eat alone in her room. Stern himself soon dissuaded her of this notion with the terse order, "I expect to see you dress for dinner, Deena."

Though shy about entering the room gowned as she had never been before, Stern's unspoken appreciation made her glow.

Dinner itself was a quiet affair with little conversation, after which Stern apologized before going off to work in his study. His abruptness disconcerted Deena and her lips tightened. Did he think she expected him to entertain her?

As the days passed, Deena settled into a certain routine. At her own insistence, she held regular teaching hours with her niece. Amy was delighted with all the attention.

"It's not as though you're some stuffy old governess, Auntie Deena," she confided one day as they walked together in one of the gardens.

Her reading and math abilities so improved that Stern couldn't help but be impressed not only with Amy's receptive intelligence, but also Deena's ability to impart knowledge.

Alone in the library one evening, Deena curled up on a green tapestry-covered paw-footed sofa. A brace of candles provided light, as did the fire crackling in the hearth of the fireplace carved with classical Greek figures and symbols. Stuffing a plush cushion behind her head, Deena savored a pamphlet she discovered on the table next to the sofa.

It had been a particularly tiring day, because Amy insisted on riding with her when she first rode out on Princess. Though a groom also rode with them, it took all Deena's tact to keep both the restless child and the skittish mare under control.

Grimacing, she thought of Amy's fall—nothing serious, but serious considering she hadn't asked Stern's permission before allowing the young girl to ride without a lead line.

Holding the pamphlet in her hand, she thought she'd handled the situation rather well. Even the groom, Esie's cheerful husband Crooks, had been complimentary.

Restlessly, she got up to study the portrait over the mantel.

The imposing full-length figure had the proud carriage of a military general; he wore his woodsman forest green clothes, moccasins, and leggings like a uniform. The arrogant face, tilted slightly to show off his distinctive beret, reminded her sharply of Stern.

Deena jumped at the sound of Stern's voice behind her. "Every one of Rogers's Rangers could hit a dollar at a hundred yards. Had to or he wasn't allowed to join."

"Who is he?" Deena asked, half expecting sarcasm.

"My grandfather." Taking Deena's arm, he led her back to the sofa. "During the French and Indian War, a man named Robert Rogers handpicked his men. Most were countrymen, hunters who fought like the Indians. It was a great honor to be considered for the Rangers."

Kyle stared at the picture a moment before staring into Deena's eyes, wide with interest. A lock of hair falling over her cheek momentarily distracted him. Absently, he tucked it behind her ear. She quivered under his touch.

Her nearness distracted him and he forced his attention back to the story. "The Rangers were in several successful skirmishes; Rogers even received a commission from the king appointing him a mayor. They were with General Wolfe in 1759. Scaled the heights of Quebec to the Plains of Abraham, taking the city and effectively ending the war.

Leastwise it was the beginning of the end."

A teasing smile played on Deena's face. "He has your arrogant bearing."

"Rhonda brings us back to earth. She always was the practical one of the family. Not a devious, nor arrogant, bone in her ample body, not like some." A frown crossed his face.

Glancing down, Stern noted the pamphlet in Deena's hand. "Reading Jonathan Edwards?"

"It is all right if I read it?"

"The library's at your disposal, Deena."

Deena flushed. "Thank you. There was not much left on our shelves when I left, what with Father selling off the books." Swinging about to face the books, Deena breathed in deeply of leather. "This is a dream come true."

Stern watched her closely. "Did you know the Reverand. Edwards said, 'God hath spoken much to you in the scripture; labor to understand as much of what he saith as you can. God hath made you all reasonable creatures, therefore let not the noble faculty of reason or understanding lie neglected.' "

Deena said, "Our vicar at home said it was important to be whatever God wants us to be. Surely then, God expects even a woman to use all the intelligence He gives her."

"Ah, a regular bluestocking, I see." He couldn't stop the hint of sarcasm.

"Father taught me to love knowledge." Deena grew pensive. "But, after Mama died, Papa was only interested in coming home to find something more to sell. Why would he give up everything he cared about for another round at the tables?"

Rubbing his forehead, Stern tried to frame an answer. "Mayhap your father was hurting inside. Mayhap he turned to that life to forget his pain."

"How could he do that without knowing how he hurt. . . others?"

"Yourself," Stern said gently. "I don't know the answer to that, Deena. I do know some people cannot see beyond their own needs and desires." For a moment bleakness crossed his face, quickly replaced with the cold reserve he used as a cover to shield his own hurt.

"I did not mean to remind you."

"Speaking for reminding, Crooks informed me you took Amy out without the lead line."

She had the grace to lower her eyes. "I'm sorry, I should have asked you first, but she was so excited about riding with me."

"When I gave you permission to ride Princess, a task in of itself, I might add, I had no idea you'd go off with Amy."

"Crooks was with us."

"True, and in that you used good judgment at least."

Deena flushed. Her eyes darkened when he added, "Amy fell."

"She wasn't hurt."

"She could have been."

"I'm sorry," Deena repeated. "But she is old enough to ride alone."

"That's *my* decision to make."

In that moment, Deena knew she'd lost whatever trust Stern might have had in her.

"I was not trying to deceive you, Mr. Stern. It was simply a spur of the moment decision. . .an err in judgment." She gulped, wondering why his opinion of her mattered so much.

Stern took a deep breath, "I fear I learned to mistrust Lizzy, and find it difficult to accept you at face value."

Deena's face flushed. "I'm not Beth. . .Lizzy."

A frown settled on Stern's lips. "Your point is well taken. Being a guardian is new to me. I want you to feel comfortable in your new home."

"Home?" This time the cynicism showed on Deena's face. "You permitted me to stay only to provide a governess for Amy."

Stern pursed his lips before speaking. "I had no idea you felt this way! I thought you liked teaching Amy. I should have recognized that you weren't ready for such responsibility."

Exasperated, Deena sighed. "I'm not too young. Maybe if you had my birth certificate you'd believe me, but then we figured my own sister would know me. And I like teaching Amy. But, you gave me to know that was the sole reason you let me stay." She could not disguise her hurt.

Leaning forward, Stern took her hand. "Mayhap I did, as you say, give that impression. Things are different now. I like your intelligence and faith. You bring sunshine and laughter into a room. You've been good for Amy. . .and me."

Deena shook her head. "Really? I didn't know. . ."

For some time after that they sat before the hearth. Its light flickered across their sometimes earnest, often laughing faces as they conversed.

"How's Princess?"

"Wonderful! She has really calmed down lately."

"Thanks to you, I've been told."

Deena smiled shyly, sobered. "Whatever happened to her?"

Stern leaned back against the cushions. "One afternoon the fool mare sailed right over the fence and galloped off into the woods. We had no idea she had that kind of ability. Actually we're not sure what happened to her. Looked like a run-in with a wolf or a bear. Somehow, she managed to limp back to the stables more dead than alive—torn, bloody, and terrified. Considered putting her down, but just could not. The physical wounds healed but she wouldn't trust anyone. . .

"Then you came along." Stern shook his head. "Jed told me, 'settled right down fer the little miss, she did.' Now, that's high praise."

Deena glanced away shyly.

This one isn't used to compliments, thought Stern. *Lord, why did she have to deceive me with Amy's riding?*

Did she really deceive you, Kyle? Is it Deena you don't trust, or your own heart?

The inner voice startled Stern so much, he stuttered. "C–Crooks did say Amy rides well."

"She does," said Deena. "Who enjoys walking an ancient pony around and around in the fence on a leading string? Past time for Amy to ride on her own."

He tented his hands. "I understand she was pretty excited

about the riding habits you ordered."

"She needed them. Besides, it makes her feel more grown up, more responsible." Deena flushed. "Oh, I didn't ask you first, did I?"

"No, you didn't." He figured her for mayhap sixteen, certainly not more. Her innocent face proclaimed her youth, though something in her eyes spoke of a certain maturity. "I suppose you claim the tendency of youth to do first and think later?" His lips twisted with pain. "Lizzy never did consider the consequences of her actions."

Deena clenched her hands. "Again, I'm not Lizzy."

"True enough." Getting up, Stern eyed the young woman with her set face. Though he fought against it, some part of him wanted to believe her. Maybe if he spent more time in her company, he'd come to know the truth. "How about riding with me in the morning?"

∾

Streaks of light had begun to stretch across the sky by the time Deena dozed off. It seemed but moments later that Esie shook her gently awake.

Impatiently, she stood while Esie helped her into one of the new habits Stern ordered for her in Portsmouth, a deep blue habit that brought out the blue in her eyes. The fitted bodice showed off her soft curves and tiny waist. Esie fastened the matching blue hat at a rakish angle on Deena's head before stepping back to admire the effect.

Deena twirled slowly before the long mirror. "Thanks, Esie."

Hurrying down the stairs, Deena tripped and landed in Stern's arms. Her cheeks flushed scarlet. "Oh!" Tears stung her eyes. "Will I never learn!"

"Learn?"

"To walk with dignified grace instead of 'scurrying about like some hoyden.'" She mimicked Margaret perfectly.

Chuckling, Stern set her down. "That, at least, is a new line."

Did he think she fell on purpose? She stared down at the toe of her new riding boots.

When Stern merely asked, "Ready?" she flashed him a ready smile, thankful he made no more of the incident

"Quite ready, Mr. Stern."

Outside, stable hands held the frisky animals already saddled and ready for exercise. Without fear Deena moved to Princess, soothing her quietly with hands and voice. Playfully, the little mare nuzzled her jacket.

At her nod, Stern threw her lightly up into the sidesaddle. As she settled, he carefully arranged her full riding skirt over the pommel. He frowned then as she handled the reins.

"Where's your riding crop? I'm sure I ordered one along with the habits."

Deena glanced at her guardian. "Yes, you did and it's lovely. But, you see, I have no need of a whip."

"I see." She warmed under the respect dawning in the eyes of her guardian.

Stern swung onto the large animal provided for him. Once more Deena proved different from her sister. He recalled with a shudder the damage Lizzy had done to one or another of his fine-blooded animals when her impatience and vicious temper led her to jerk the reins, kick the animal, and beat the poor creature about the head and neck with her whip.

It did not take long to discover that, unlike Lizzy, Deena was not only an expert horsewoman, but immensely patient with the skittish little mare.

Sometime later, Stern pulled up at a long stretch of level ground and pointed. "See that large white pine in the middle of the gallop ahead?"

The tall trees, standing like spectators awaiting a race, marched on either side of a wide cleared strip of land. Beside Stern, Deena shaded her eyes. "I see."

"Good. I'll race you to the tree." He grinned. "At least the jumps aren't set out right now or you'd leave us behind." He patted the thick neck of his roan. "This one is no jumper."

"Ah, too bad." Deena hunched down over the saddle as Stern counted.

"One. Two. Three. Go!" The little mare jumped to the lead.

Deena grinned back at the startled face of her guardian.

With a deep grunt, the roan surged forward, eating up the little mare's slim lead. Leaning forward, Deena encouraged Princess, who eagerly responded, her ears flicking back to heed her rider's commands.

Stern grinned back at her as he urged on the roan, then sobered as he saw Deena once more talk to the mare and the mare once more respond. However much he tried, he could not lengthen his lead.

The mare strained forward, her breaths heavy and white in the morning chill. Once more the roan surged ahead. From somewhere the mare found more reserve and hung on the roan's tail. They passed the tree in a blur, leaving it behind as both Deena and Stern slowly eased the horses to a canter, to a walk. For a long time they let the animals cool, riding in comfortable, silent, companionship.

The gallop was long passed, the wood gave way to rolling green fields. Topping a small rise they looked down over the vista spread out before them in neat cultivated squares.

"It's beautiful," breathed Deena. "Yours?"

"Three Oaks ends at the river. That's EverPine and it belongs to—" Suddenly he tensed, his gaze riveted below him to a woman riding a white horse.

seven

Heedless of his ward, Stern swung the roan about and galloped in the opposite direction. So intent were his thoughts,
Stern scarcely noted the confused young woman at his side.
Why did Helen have to return now when contentment seemed
within his grasp? His scowl deepened.

Mentally he shook himself, trying to shake off his sense of
dread. He should be glad she was back. She was, after all, a
good friend. He wanted Deena to. . .Deena!

With a groan he pulled the roan to a halt and looked down
into the flashing eyes of his ward. "I owe you an apology. I
was surprised that my neighbor Helen Billings returned without notice."

Deena winced. "You're close to the woman?"

"I help manage her estate." Stern paused, feeling he owed
Deena an explanation. "Helen and Lizzy were close friends.
In truth, Helen was with Lizzy those last days. When her own
husband died soon after. . ." Stern shrugged.

"Besides, Amy needed a woman about. Helen has been
good about managing the household."

"I see." Deena said in a tight voice. "She's your fiancée?"

"I will thank you, Miss Heyford," said Stern repressively,
"to keep from starting rumors."

Deena flared. "I'm not. Why can't you trust me?""

Leaping to the ground, Stern lifted Deena from the mare's
back. She winced as her weak leg hit the ground. "Young
lady, I have had quite enough of that saucy tongue of yours.
Curb that temper or I'll take you over my knee."

Deena gasped, hiccuped. Eyes wide, she stared up at the
giant looming over her.

At Deena's response, Stern continued more gently. "I'm
sorry. . .again, but like it or not, I am also your guardian and I

will not countenance disrespect. Is that clear!" From the way she flinched, he knew he was intimidating her and felt a twinge of guilt.

"I understand, *Mr. Stern.*" Deena blinked rapidly.

He asked unsteadily, "Did I hurt you?" Her bones felt so fragile under his grasp.

"Just scared the wits out of me." She patted the nose of the inquiring mare, who nuzzled her anxiously. "I'm all right, Princess."

The set down had not gone as expected and Stern stood nonplused, angry, mostly at himself. "Let me help you." Deftly, he reseated Deena onto the mare.

Lord, I think I'm beginning to care for her. She's so young and, though I don't want to, I think I'm beginning to believe in her. What am I to do?

Almost, he thought he sensed his Heavenly Father smile.

Overhead, the morning clouds broke and a warm spring sun beamed down on them. The only sound was the steady clop-clop of the horses' hooves on the path. From the tall pines waiting like dark sentinels standing at attention on the left, Deena heard the trill of brightly colored birds. Far off came the dying screech of some small animal.

"The trees are very beautiful," she spoke to take her mind from the silence and sudden death. "They remind me of church steeples or ship's masts."

"Funny you should say that. So happens these trees make the best white pine masts in the world."

"So that's how you got into the business."

"Not me personally, New Hampshire, though you can see, just by looking around, how my family made its fortune. First we built ships, then sailed them. Rhonda's husband takes care of the building side now."

He paused. Deena's interest spurred him on. "Long before our independence, English seamen came here for their masts. Often we ended up building the whole ship. One of grandfather's rivals built the Ranger for John Paul Jones."

"I've heard of him. His ships did the British much damage

in the war for independence."

Stern smiled then. "The British. Have you decided to throw in your lot with us, *Lady* Heyford?"

Deena stilled her retort at the teasing light in the eyes of her guardian. "I don't know. Mayhap I don't belong anywhere anymore." The words trailed off.

"You belong here, Deena. Amy needs you. I do too. Then there's Helen. She'll welcome you with open arms."

Thinking of the veiled warnings she'd heard about this Helen Billings, Deena wondered at Stern's optimism.

The meeting was not long in coming. That same afternoon Stern called her and Amy from their afternoon walk. As the two paused outside the French doors, Amy gripped Deena's hand.

"I don't wanta go in," she whispered.

Deena stopped, wiped a smudge from Amy's cheek. "We must. Your father asked for us."

Amy pouted. "I don't wanta see her now."

Deena's eyes widened. "You mean Mrs. Billings? Hasn't she given you dolls and other nice things?"

Amy sniffed. "Yes, but. . ."

"We must be polite to the guest."

"She's no guest!" To Deena's chagrin, the little girl wiped a grimy hand on her yellow gown, leaving a telltale black smear. "Now that she's back, she'll be here all the time."

"Enough, Amy!" Deena tried to hide her dismay from the sharp-eyed little girl. "We're going in and we *shall* be on our best behavior!"

"Yes, Auntie Deena." Amy took her aunt's hand with unusual submissiveness.

Together, they approached the couple sitting on the velvet-covered couch. Stern leaned away from the lovely lady sitting beside him. Annoyance crossed the lady's face, quickly replaced by an indulgent smile.

"Amy dear, come here," she cooed.

Amy froze and Deena gave her a nudge. Reluctantly, Amy moved forward and stiffly accepted a quick hug. "Why Amy, what's this? Your dress is filthy and your face!"

She smoothed her gown. "I can see it's about time I returned."

Crimson flooded Deena's pale cheeks. "Ma'am, if we'd had time, we would have changed."

A high tinkling laugh fell from Helen's full red lips. Tendrils of red hair framed Helen's cream complexion, lending an artful casualness to her carefully arranged coiffured hair. Her green eyes surveyed Deena.

"Is this is your little ward, Kyle?"

Deena watched as Stern's gaze strayed to her hair which, escaping from its long braid, hung down her back in silvery waves.

Something akin to pain flashed in Helen's eyes. "How remiss of us, Kyle. Run along and change, dears."

Though the woman's tone was kind enough, Deena bit back a retort at once more being classified as a child, and a tiresome one at that. Glancing toward her guardian for instructions, Deena's heart skidded at the trusting expression on his face as he gazed at Helen. If only he'd look at her with such trust.

"Can we go?" Amy, shifting from one foot to another, asked plaintively.

Stern held out his arms. "Give Papa a hug first."

With a tight smile, Helen moved over as Amy jumped into her father's arms and plied him with kisses. After a bear hug, Amy ran out of the room. Deena turned to follow, but Stern patted the open place beside him.

"Sit down, Deena. Join us for tea. I'd like you and Helen to get better acquainted."

Warming in his smile, Deena gingerly sat down.

"Kyle, we mustn't embarrass the girl. Dear, if you'd like to change first. . ." Helen smiled. Deena smiled back.

"Time for that later, Helen. Miss Heyford, may I make you formally acquainted with Helen Billings. Helen, Deena."

"Kyle, surely you don't make this child work."

"Miss Heyford isn't a child, Helen, but a young woman."

His eyes twinkled, "As she often reminds me."

On a large silver salver, Bailey brought in tea, lemonade, and a host of tiny sandwiches and sweets. Helen poured out the drinks and distributed the afternoon repast with all the dignity of a gracious English hostess.

"Deena?" Lost in her own thoughts, Deena had all but forgotten Stern and Helen.

"Pardon? I fear I was thinking of how like this is to home."

"This is home now, Deena," Stern said. "Helen, Deena can be a great help to you in managing the house. Fact is, I hope that soon she'll be able to lift the burden of our household from your shoulders. She is young, but willing to learn."

Deena glowed in his warm approval.

Helen's long fingers on Stern's arm refocused his attention once more onto her. "It's no burden, Kyle. What with Ralph gone these past three years." Stern patted her arm as she paused with a strangled sob that wrenched Deena's soft heart.

"My place is so empty, barren, without husband or children."

Stern disentangled his arm from her stranglehold. "Helen, I'm not trying to get rid of you, but now that Deena's here. . .I just thought. . ." His gaze strayed to Deena.

Helen wiped her nose on a delicate linen square and sniffed, "Forgive me, Kyle. But helping you has never been a burden." She leaned over to tap Deena's knee. "Please don't take offense, dear, of course Kyle wants you to learn to manage the household. It's something every gently brought up female needs to learn." She paused. "Of course I'll teach you how to get along."

"Thank you, Mrs. Billings," said Deena, hiding her frustration. The woman was only being kind, after all, and this was no time to explain she'd managed her father's household, such as it was, after the death of her mother.

However, Deena soon discovered that while Helen spent more time at Three Oaks than she did at her own home, she left most of the household management in the hands of the housekeeper, Mrs. Bitley. Furthermore, Mrs. Bitley brooked no interference in the running of the house, and she'd taken a particular dislike to Deena.

More and more Deena and Amy found excuses to leave the oppressive house. They rode together, they walked in the gardens, and usually did their lessons out-of-doors.

One morning while reading *The Adventures of Robin Hood* to Amy, Deena momentarily glanced up toward the house. From the French door of the parlor, Helen stared out at them. Deena winced at the glare of hatred twisting the woman's face.

When Deena looked again, the look had been replaced by one of benign concern. Deena shook herself. Surely what she had seen had been but a trick of light.

"Amy, dear," Helen called. "I'd like to see you."

Deena stood to follow. "No, Deena, just Amy."

She added, "Want to go for a drive in my new gig?"

Amy's face brightened at the thought. Still, she hesitated until Deena gave her a mild shove. "Go on, have fun. We'll start again tomorrow."

Deena entered the house slowly, her footsteps echoing hollowly on the inlaid floor. How did Helen find so much to do in a house dominated by the ever-present Mrs. Bitley?

Esie snorted at the question. "One reason only, Missy. Be the master himself, that one is after." That had been the morning before. Deena had not seen the cheerful maid hence.

Suddenly, Mrs. Bitley's solid bulk barred Deena's way. Disconcerted, Deena quickly gathered her wits. Mustering her most authoritative tone, she asked. "I'm going to my room."

Mrs. Bitley did not move. "When last did you see Esie?"

Deena licked her lips. She had no wish to trouble the maid who had befriended her. "Why do you want her?"

At the smirk on the woman's face, Deena knew her evasive answer had given the housekeeper the answer. "I take it you have not seen her on duty for some time. . .Miss Heyford." The woman's attitude bordered on insolence.

Anger flashed in Deena's eyes. "Is that all, Mrs. Bitley?" She made as though to pass the woman. Eyes mocking, the housekeeper stepped aside, slowly.

Still angry, Deena stamped up the stairs, then groaned as her leg gave. Pitching forward, Deena frantically grabbed the banister to keep herself from falling. Trembling at her close call, Deena lowered herself on the stairs.

Glancing below her, she caught a flash of disappointment in the eyes of the housekeeper before the woman marched away. Why had the housekeeper made no attempt to help her?

Firmly grasping the rail, Deena hurried up to the safety of her chamber. After ringing for Esie, she tried to rid herself of her feeling of dread. "Dear Lord, help me."

To her surprise, a tall, thin girl answered the summons. "I'm Jeana." Reluctantly, the girl curtsied.

"Where's Esie?" Deena demanded.

"Gone."

"Gone!" echoed Deena. "Where? Why?"

Jeana shrugged. Grabbing her arm, Deena forced the girl to face her. "What happened to Esie?"

Sullenly Jeana pulled away. "Mrs. Bitley, she fire 'er."

Color drained from Deena 's face. "Tell Mrs. Bitley I wish to see her, right here, right now!" When Jeana hesitated, Deena started toward the girl. "Do as I say. . .now!"

Hatred flashed in the girl's eyes, but she did as she was bid. Deena closed her eyes, rubbed her leg, which still ached from her near fall on the stairs.

By the time the housekeeper deigned to make her appearance almost an hour later, Deena was in a fine state.

"What did you do to Esie?" she snapped.

Mrs. Bitley stiffened at Deena's tone. "Esie has not been adoin' her job, as you well know. I sent her and that good fer nothin' husband of hers apackin'."

"Crooks is a perfectly capable groom and you know it."

"Cain't 'ave a maid not adoin' 'er job." Mrs. Bitley's face was set, hard.

Taking a deep breath, Deena calmed herself. "Where is she?"

Hesitantly, as though the words were dragged from between

her clenched teeth, Mrs. Bitley answered. "Packin' in 'er quarters." She added. "Might already be gone."

"You may go now, Mrs. Bitley, but do not think you've heard the end of this."

Waiting until the housekeeper's heavy footsteps faded down the hall, Deena hastened down the back staircase to the servant's quarters. Deena found Esie in her bedchamber. Tears coursed down the woman's cheeks as she slowly packed. Nearby, a toddler lay on a bed.

"Esie." Startled, Esie wiped tears from her eyes. "I just heard. Esie, what's wrong?"

Esie turned away. "Nothing you can do, missy. My man and I be gone by afternoon."

"Stuff and feathers! You're not going anywhere until I know what happened!" Deena felt her temper rise.

Wearily, she motioned for Deena to join her at the side of the bed. A small child lay unnaturally still in the large bed, her face flushed with fever. A shiver caught her, making her blond curls dance about her damp cheeks. "Mama, Mama," cried the child.

Deena touched the child's forehead. "She's burning up. What has been done for her?"

"I've been nursin' her myself."

"A doctor?"

Esie shook her head. "Mrs. Bitley says a doctor's not for the likes of us. Missy, I couldn't leave my baby. I couldn't!" Her voice broke.

"Of course you couldn't! Esie, don't you dare go anywhere. I'm getting a doctor."

At the door, Deena asked, "Did Helen. . .Mrs. Billings know about this?"

Esie shrugged. "Cain't say, missy."

"I see. You'll stay."

Esie nodded.

Outside the little bedroom, Deena leaned wearily against the wall and closed her eyes. "Lord, help me know what to do. Help me not to fail."

Her first thought was to find Helen, but she had taken Amy with her for a ride in the new gig she'd recently purchased.

Stern. Right! She had to find Stern. He was the only one who could override the housekeeper's pronouncement.

At the stables, Deena found Esie's usually cheerful husband grim. "Crooks, saddle Princess immediately."

"Yes, missy." Not long thereafter he brought around the little mare and lifted Deena into the saddle.

Lifting the reins, Deena said. "Crooks, I need to find Mr. Stern. Where is he this morning?"

"Over on the far forty."

"Thanks. And Crooks, stop worrying and don't leave until I speak to my guardian."

Hope shone in Dale's eyes. "Godspeed, missy."

Away from the stables, Deena reined in to get her bearings. She was glad she had gained knowledge of the layout of the land on her rides with Stern. About half an hour later she caught up with him.

Deep in conversation with his manager, Stern frowned as Deena rode up. "Deena?"

The manager, whose name she could not recall, acknowledged her with a nod. "Miss Heyford." He glanced toward Stern.

"Mr. Stern, I need to speak with you. It's urgent." Her eyes pleaded.

"All right. We'll be finished in an hour or so. Then I'll ride back with you."

Deena bit her lip. Tears stung her eyes. "Mr. Stern." She cleared her throat. "This cannot wait." Snorting, Princess shifted skittishly, reflecting his mistress's agitation.

Annoyance crossed Stern's face. "What's wrong?"

Deena's eyes flashed. "Nellie's sick."

"Crooks's little girl? Send for a doctor, then."

Deena sucked in a breath, her anger fading. "You didn't forbid it?"

"What nonsense." Anger flashed in Stern's eyes.

Slowly, Deena explained and had the satisfaction of seeing

his face flush. "Are you saying that Mrs. Bitley not only denied the child medical services, but also fired both Esie and Dale?"

" 'Tis all true. I found Esie packing. I've seen Nellie. She's very ill."

A mask settled over Stern's face, only this time Deena sensed he used it to maintain self-control. He turned to the manager. "I'll leave you to finish here. Come see me, say eight in the morning, to discuss your conclusions. Come, Deena."

At the entrance of the mansion he slid off the tall roan and threw the reins to a young lad who ran forward. Impatiently, he lifted Deena from her saddle and assisted her up the stairs at a pace she would not have managed by herself.

"Bailey," he all but bellowed. "I want to see Mrs. Bitley immediately in my study. Get the doctor for Crooks's little girl. Oh, and let them know they are definitely staying on." Striding toward his study, Stern angrily slapped his riding crop against his dusty riding boots.

As Bailey left to do Stern's bidding, Deena smiled and walked toward Amy, who stared at her from the bottom step. "Amy."

The child pouted belligerently. "Thought you loved me, Auntie Deena."

Deena sat down beside her. "I do, Amy. Very much."

"Why do you want ta go away?"

Deena sucked in a deep breath. "Amy, I have no idea what you're talking about." At Amy's hesitation, Deena took the girl's hand. "Let's talk in the library," she suggested, not adding, "so Mrs. Bitley won't interrupt us."

Silently, Amy sat beside Deena on a sofa in the book room. "Now, Amy."

Amy's legs dangled. She wriggled uncomfortably. "Mrs. Billings says you might go away to school."

Hurt shone in the girl's eyes. "Don't leave me, Auntie Deena. Please!"

Deena closed her eyes. Was Stern so soon tired of her? "Amy, believe me. This is the first I've heard of this. I think we need speak to your father about this, don't you? You don't believe he'd lie to you, do you?"

Lowering her eyes, Amy shook her head. A moment later, she jumped off the sofa. "Come, Auntie Deena, let's see him now."

Following her, Deena completely forgot about Stern's imminent meeting with the housekeeper and boldly knocked at the study door.

The door opened in her face. Deena backed away as the housekeeper, her face distorted with hate, pushed passed her. "On yer high horse, are ya?" she hissed. "Not fer long."

Gulping, Deena gingerly stuck her head into the study. After a run-in with the housekeeper, she dreaded another set-to with her guardian.

Amy ran in. "Papa. Papa! Deena has something important to ask you."

Stern saw her hesitating at the threshold. "Come in, Deena." He sounded tired.

As he pulled Amy onto his lap, Deena took a seat on a deep-cushioned chair before the large oak desk strewn with papers, quills, a chased ink pot, and several large volumes.

Amy put her chubby arms about her father's neck. "What's so important?" He looked from his solemn daughter to his weary ward.

Amy did not wait for Deena to speak. "Oh, Papa. Don't send Auntie Deena away. Please don't send her away!"

"This some kind of jest?" He frowned.

Deena shook her head bleakly. Amy pulled his attention back to her. "Miz Billings says you're gonna send Auntie Deena away to school."

Suspicion lurked in the dark eyes surveying Deena. "Nonsense. Why would Helen tell you such a noddy-cocked thing?"

"You mean you're not planning to ship me off to some young woman's seminary?"

"Of course not! True, Helen and I talked about it. She thought you would rather be with girls your own age." He paused. "Are you lonely?"

"Certainly not! I don't want to leave Amy, or Three Oaks, or. . ." Her eyes widened as she recognized the truth of the matter.

"Auntie Deena gonna stay, Papa?"

Stern hugged his daughter. "Of course she's going to stay. I don't think we can do without her, do you?" His smile drew an answering smile from Deena. Relief showed in her gray eyes.

"As for Nellie, she'll be taken care of."

"Mrs. Bitley is extremely angry with me."

"Don't let that concern you, Deena." His eyes were cold. "I asked her to leave."

The news staggered her. "Truly?"

"I fear I have let things run on too long as it is. I knew some of the servants thought her rather hard and unfeeling. Put it off as the usual sort of grumbling that goes on, until today. I'm glad you came to me." His gaze warmed her clear to her toes. "You are a godsend to us, Deena, a godsend."

Deena flushed, bit her lip. "I couldn't believe anyone would treat a sick child like that."

"I know. She's good at what she does and she's good at nursing, too, but, it seems only toward those she cares about. She nursed her husband before he passed on." He sighed. "Took her on because Helen felt sorry for her." His face hardened. "But I'll not countenance such deliberate cruelty to a child."

For a moment no one spoke as he deliberated. "Deena," he said slowly, "Esie and Dale both speak well of you, as do the other servants. Seems you have a facility for engendering loyalty and respect among the staff." He smiled down at Amy. "In young children as well."

He rubbed his chin. "Would you consider taking on the running of the household? Three Oaks cannot be much larger than your father's home in England."

"Are you hiring me for Mrs. Bitley's job?" She could not hide her disappointment.

Stern hastened to correct her. "Not at all, my dear." The endearment slipped out unnoticed. "I want you to hire the new housekeeper. I think you have a sense of what's needed. I'd feel better knowing the household is running smoothly."

"Thank you." Deena's eyes brightened, then dimmed. "What about Mrs. Billings?"

"Despite what she says, I believe Helen has enough to do. Of course, we'll go into this gradually as she instructs you."

Deena's lips tightened.

"Surely you're not jealous of Helen."

Deena sighed. Was she jealous? *Lord, forgive me.* "When do you wish me to begin, sir?"

Stern frowned. "If you don't want to take over, say so."

"I do want the job, I do," Deena said. "Does that mean I have the authority to hire. . .and release servants?"

"With my approval, of course." He put Amy on his shoulder. As he stood, Amy screeched her delight at being so tall. "Let's discuss the details over the luncheon."

Exhausted after the physical and emotional exertions of the morning, Deena, at Stern's command, dragged up to her room after lunch for a long nap. His concern brought tears to her eyes. What a paradox was the man.

Thinking only of her comfortable bed, Deena entered her room only to be brought up short by Helen Billings.

"Deena, dear. Why didn't you come to me with your complaint instead of running off to Kyle? I could have straightened things out with Mrs. Bitley."

"I would have, Mrs. Billings, but you were off with Amy, and Nellie needed help."

"I hate to see her lose her job over this." Helen sucked in a deep breath.

"I'm sorry, really I am, since I know she got the job on your recommendation." Deena shook her head. "But Three Oaks is well shed of a woman who denies a child medical attention."

"I agree she made a dreadful mistake." Helen paused, as though gathering her self-control. Her voice low and soft, she said, "Am I to understand you'll be leaving us to attend school?" Again she paused, cleared her throat. "I'll miss you, Deena."

"You won't miss me, Helen."

Helen's eyes narrowed. "No?"

Deena grinned. "I meant no offense, Helen. It's just that my guardian assured me I won't be sent away unless I wish it, and I do not. The Crookses are also staying."

"What of poor Mrs. Bitley? What is she going to do?" Helen sighed. "She can't afford to be without work. I know what she did was unforgivable, but. . ."

Deena felt herself weaken. *Lord?* She smiled at the answer that presented itself. "I've got it, Helen. Didn't you mention losing your housekeeper recently? Hire Mrs. Bitley. At EverPine you can keep an eye on her."

Helen's cheeks reddened to match her exquisitely coiffured hair. "You might ask Kyle to take her back. He'll listen to you."

"I'd rather not, Helen. She doesn't get along with the staff, but might do better for you. It seems she looks up to you." Deena hated to disappoint Stern's friend. "Actually, I plan to promote Esie to the job."

"You!" Helen's voice rose. "If anyone decides who replaces Mrs. Bitley, it will be me." Deena stepped back at Helen's unexpected vehemence.

"I've learned enough to manage now. Mr. Stern agrees that I'm ready to take over the duties of the household, including the replacement of the housekeeper." Deena softened the obvious blow to Mrs. Billings. "With your advice and support, of course."

Helen choked, coughed. "Of course, dear. You don't mind if I discuss this with Kyle, do you? After all, you are awfully young."

Deena had enough of this child thing. "No, I'm not all that young, Helen. I'm nineteen and quite old enough to manage the household."

Lips tight, Helen left the room, leaving a distinct chill behind.

eight

Sitting stiff and straight on the very edge of her dresser chair, Deena waited for a summons from Stern, fully expecting to be summarily packed off to the nearest boarding school while Helen resumed full control of the household at Three Oaks. Her prayer was as jumbled as her confusing emotions.

"Help me stay, Lord. I don't want to leave. . .Kyle." The words, finally admitted, came out in a rush.

Even in the privacy of her room, she blushed. However had she developed a tendresse for her difficult guardian? The man harassed her with ridiculous accusations and suspicions that infuriated her.

She smiled softly, recalling his gentleness after Clyde's attack, other times, too. 'Twas not to finishing school they should be sending her, but to Bedlam!

Downstairs, Helen tensed at Stern's determination. "No, Helen, you misunderstood. Sending Deena away to school was a suggestion only, but she doesn't wish to go. I think she feels too old. Besides, I gave my word, and I shall keep it. She's good for Amy. Furthermore, from what I understand from Esie, she did manage her father's household."

Helen leaned closer to Stern on the long, overstuffed sofa. "Deena's young; I'd hate to see her break under the burden of managing your household."

Even Deena's name warmed his cold heart. "I see your point, but you'll be here to guide her."

Helen nodded. "I'll be here as long as I'm needed. You won't get rid of me that easily."

Stern chuckled, but felt he needed to make his point. "Make no mistake, Helen, I consider Deena as part of my family. Sending her off now would only convince her I wished to be rid of her." Beside him, Helen tensed. "Besides, I promised to keep Porter from her. I can do that best right here."

"Clyde. Has your ward already developed an unhealthy partiality?"

"Enough!" Helen flinched at his vehemence. "The man quite frightened her out of her wits."

"Mayhap he sees a bit of Lizzy in her?" Helen suggested, then bit her lip at Stern's thunderous frown. "I'm sorry, Kyle. Of course we must do what is best for her."

Absently, Stern patted her hand. "You've been a good friend." So saying, he stood. "If you will excuse me."

≈

When no summons came, Deena relaxed. If anything, in the next days, her guardian was more considerate than before. In fact, things were almost idyllic, especially since Helen seemed most anxious to show Deena how to manage the staff.

Stern's new confidence in Deena manifested itself in her increased self-confidence. Deena smiled more often, withdrew less. More than once, Helen mentioned the need for Deena to have friends of her same age, but even she was forced to admit the girl had a flare for organization. Deena felt she and Helen were growing close.

Deena sent Jeana back to her home and promoted Esie. With proper medical attention, Nellie recovered quickly, leaving Esie free to concentrate on her new duties. Within days, the whole atmosphere of Three Oaks changed. Often, Deena heard humming as the maids went about their duties, laughter from the servants' hall.

"The staff is happier," commented Stern, "I've never seen them work with more efficiency."

She glowed under his praise. "Esie brings out the best in them, sir."

He patted her shoulder. "Maybe so, but it was your idea to give her the job. How is your new maid working out?"

Deena smiled. "Esie's cousin Enid? She's a delight."

Deena was happier than she had been in some time. Stern had not railed at her for days. Even Helen seemed to accept her position in the household.

"Mrs. Bitley is doing well at EverPine," she told Deena, patting her hand. "You had a good idea there." She smiled. "We've become friends, have we not?"

"I'd like to think so."

"Good, I think so, too." Helen sipped her tea. "I know Kyle isn't always the easiest man to get along with." Deena refrained from rolling her eyes as Helen continued. "But I can handle him. So if you ever have any problems, come to me."

Deena grinned. "Thanks, I appreciate it, Helen." If only she could be as comfortable with her guardian.

Margaret, she wrote that evening.

Impossible as it seems, my guardian even laughs once in a while now. Amy is a dear. And the neighbor, Helen Billings, has become my friend. She spends much of her time at Three Oaks. My guardian says since she's all alone, she feels more useful here.

The other day we visited her place. I think she likes my guardian, but I'm not sure her feelings are returned. I had the vague impression she would have preferred it to be a tête-à-tête, just she and Stern, but he prefers the presence of his family. Has a nice sound, doesn't it?

Hope you and Orrin are well.

My Regards

She wasn't about to confess she had feelings for her tall guardian as well. Those she kept well hidden, deep inside.

The morning dawned chill, the clouds threatened rain. Though Deena covered her habit with a wool cape, as Enid had insisted, the wind kept whipping it aside, permitting the chill air to swirl around her.

"You're chilled. Mayhap we should cut our ride short."

As Deena shook her head, her hat flew away and her hair, loosened by the wind, tumbled down about her shoulders in a profusion of silver.

Stern sucked in a breath. Of its own accord, his hand reached out to stroke her hair. He pulled it back sharply.

Puzzled at his strange action, Deena stared up at him. The teasing retort on her lips died suddenly as they gazed into each other's eyes. The world around them faded, and for that moment, there was only the two of them.

A fluttering leaf made Princess dance skittishly. Hastily, Deena grabbed the reins to settle the mare. She felt drained.

"Let's ride," said Stern gruffly, pulling his roan about.

Silently, Deena followed, feeling her own heart beat in time to Princess's hooves. As Stern lengthened his lead, Deena drank in the commanding figure of her guardian. To the side, the wind moaned through the tall trees.

Suddenly she heard a loud snap as a large white pine swayed and began to fall. Faster and faster it fell, as Princess reared in panic.

Hauling around the roan, Stern reached back, snatched Deena from the saddle, and kicked the roan into a gallop just as the tree crashed down across the path.

Deena clutched Stern's jacket as behind her Princess screamed. Then they heard only the moaning wind. Stern held Deena tightly to him in the front of the saddle. "Deena, my dear, are you all right?"

"Princess," Deena sobbed, her head against her guardian's wide shoulders.

Stern looked down at the slight figure snuggling in his arms as though she belonged there. Gently, he lifted her tearstained white face to his. Shock in the wide gray eyes stabbed through the coldness surrounding his heart, leaving him vulnerable. Lowering the reins, Stern gathered Deena to him, rocking her back and forth in his arms.

Raising his hand, he brushed damp silver strands from her face, his chest tightening at the feel of the silken loveliness cascading over his hand.

"My dearest Deena, you're safe. Praise God!"

"Princess!" Deena shivered in Stern's arms, and he held her close as rain began to fall. Whipped by the wind, the drops pelted them with the sting of a whip.

Pulling his caped coat about the shivering girl who had

somehow found a place in his shuttered heart, Stern headed
the gallant roan into the wall of wind and rain. With effort
the fine animal picked his way back to the stables.

Sliding off with Deena in his arms, Stern strode into the
stables. Crooks followed with the dripping roan.

"Esie be frantic," he called. " 'Bout ready ta cum after ya."

After setting Deena on a large box, Stern mopped her
streaming face. He motioned for Crooks.

"Miss Heyford's horse is still out there," he said, giving a
terse summary of events.

Crooks paled. "Esie, she knows somethin' be wrong. She
be aprayin'."

His kind eyes settled on the miserable Deena. "I'll be
aseein' about the mare as soon as the rain lets up."

"Good. But Crooks, I don't want you risking your neck
understood?"

Reluctantly, Crooks nodded.

Walking to the front of the stables, Stern looked toward the
manor, obscured by the wind and rain. "I fear, Deena, we're
trapped here for the time being."

Stern frowned as Deena shivered in her wet clothes. Pulling
off his heavy cape, he was about to wrap it about her when
Crooks handed him a horse blanket, which he substituted.
Drowsily, Deena leaned against the wall.

Some two hours later, when the rain eased, Stern gathered
Deena in his strong arms and sprinted toward the house. Once
inside, he headed up the stairs to Deena's chamber with Esie
hustling up behind him.

After having a warm bath and changing into a nightgown
Deena let Esie tuck her under the covers.

"Ya be all right now, missy." Esie fluffed the pillow behind
Deena's head. "You just rest awhile."

"What about Amy? Luncheon?"

"Amy's fine now that she knows you're all right. As for
luncheon, we'll just put it off a bit. I'll send Enid up in time
to get ya ready." Closing the drapes, Esie firmly left the
room.

Deena smiled. Images of Stern's comforting arms pervaded her drifting thoughts.

ॐ

As she entered the anteroom to the dining hall, Amy hugged her. "Auntie Deena, I was so scared for you."

"I'm all right, Amy. God kept me and your father safe." Her eyes met those of her guardian, who was surveying her questioningly.

"Truly, I am fine." She blushed, lowered her eyes to her charge. "Thanks to your father."

As Deena dramatically retold the story of her rescue, Amy stared at her father adoringly. "Papa, you're wonderful. You saved Auntie Deena!"

Stern protested, but to no avail. Deena's eyes twinkled mischievously. "Am I not telling it correctly, sir?"

"Quite puts me to the blush," he teased. At the tenderness in his gaze, it was Deena who blushed.

They ate in companionable silence. Deena almost felt they *were* family.

Suddenly, Amy raised her head, frowned. "It's so quiet."

"Too quiet," said Deena.

"The rain has stopped." Esie spoke at Stern's elbow. "Dale'll be ariding out to see about the mare now."

Nodding, Stern rose from the table. "If you ladies will excuse me, I'll think I'll ride along." He looked at Deena. "We'll bring her back if we can," he promised.

As he left, Deena took Amy's hand firmly and led her to the library. "We have work to do, young lady. I fear this morning put us behind in your studies."

They sat down at the desk. Opening the large leather-covered Bible, Deena indicated a passage, "Read this verse from Psalm 118:6."

Following along with her finger, Amy read slowly, "The Lord is on my side; I will not fear: what can man do unto me?"

"Very good." Deena hugged the little girl, whom she'd come to love as her own. "No matter what happens, we can trust God to take care us," she explained. Pointing, she asked,

"See this mark at the end of the sentence?"

Bailey, clearing his throat, interrupted the session. "Umm. Mrs. Billings would like a word with you, Miss Heyford."

Helen moved gracefully into the room. Seeing Amy, she stopped. Something Deena couldn't identify flickered across her face. Then she smiled. "Amy, run along to Mrs. Cairns. I have a surprise for your aunt."

Helen waited until both Amy and Bailey left the room. "An old friend dropped by last night. He asked after you."

"I know of no one. . .perhaps for Mr. Stern."

"Indeed not. This gentlemen particularly wished to see you." She watched Deena closely.

"Time to come in?"

Deena shuddered as Clyde Porter bowed smartly. "Mr. Porter!" Deena managed through the fear rising in her throat.

Though she didn't offer him her hand, he appropriated it anyway. "I said I'd come."

Helen clasped her hands. "Isn't this cozy? Clyde has been a dear friend for years. How wonderful he finds time to attend you, Deena." Her chatter set Deena's teeth on edge.

Glancing up at the taller woman, Deena tried to explain the truth of the matter, but Helen didn't seem to understand.

Helen smiled. "Isn't it lovely that we're all such goood friends? Dear, I do have to see Esie about tea. You two go on and visit. I'll be back as soon as possible." She flashed Clyde a look of apology. "With all that rain, I'm afraid Kyle won't return for hours."

"Helen, you don't understand," Deena stammered, but found herself talking to the woman's retreating figure. The door closed with a decided *click!*

As Deena headed toward the door, Clyde swung her about so quickly she fell. "Getting restive for my attentions, are we, little one?"

"Release me this instant! My guardian—"

"Is occupied elsewhere. By the time he returns, it will be far too late."

Deena stiffened. "The servants."

"They're all well occupied in another area of the house. Large houses are so very convenient for a bit of dallying, don't you think?" He pulled her roughly down beside him on the green-covered couch.

"Lord, help me. Kyle!" She screamed. Surely someone would hear, surely someone would come.

"Not again, little Deena." His mouth covered hers.

When he finally released her, Deena wiped her sore mouth. Tears stung her eyes. Instinctively, Deena slapped him. Grabbing her hands, he pulled her to him.

"When I am finished with you, little Deena, no self-respecting man will shelter you."

"You wouldn't dare."

Porter laughed as he forced her back against the cushions. "It matters not whether or not you submit willingly, the result will be the same. Besides, I'll just explain you asked me to meet you. . .in private."

"I didn't! Let me go!" She screamed again as his hands roamed. "Why?" she asked as nausea heaved her stomach.

"You toyed with me, just as did your sister."

"I didn't!"

"Ah, but you've come between Helen and Stern."

Deena went limp. Her action put Clyde off a moment, a moment Deena used to fling herself from the couch. Porter gave her no time to crawl away.

His body pressed down on hers, his lips smothered hers. Desperately, she fought as tears streamed down her cheeks.

Suddenly long arms yanked Porter to his feet. "You dare attack my ward in my home!"

For but a moment fear flashed in Porter's eyes, then he smirked. "You know how it is, old chap. I was asked to attend the young miss in private. We all understand about these things." He had the nerve to wink at Deena, who turned away.

Stern took in Deena's white face, her tearstained cheeks.

She flinched as Porter sneered, "Just like her sister, she is."

"Get out, Clyde. Get out while you still have working legs." Stern spoke with chilling menace. "Consider my earlier promise now fulfilled."

Porter's face paled. At the door, he turned. "I'll leave the wench to you, Stern, but heed this. There is talk already of the lovely young woman living unchaperoned at Three Oaks."

"Deena is my sister-in-law."

"But her guardian is unmarried, and though young, the maiden could still be considered fair game, especially by anyone who knew of her sister." With a leer at Deena, Porter closed the door.

Stern looked deep into eyes glazed with shock and hurt. There was no pretense in the terrorized gaze nor in the shivers he recalled had been her response after the last assault.

Lord, how could I ever have suspected her of complicity in this? Sitting beside her, Stern spoke softly. "Deena. Deena."

Carefully, he slipped an arm about her tense body and forced her head against his shoulder.

"I'm here now, Deena. Clyde is gone. You're safe."

Stern tried again. "Deena, did you invite him?"

For some time he continued in this vein before sensing a response. Then great sobs broke forth from his ward and tears streamed down her white cheeks. Stern tightened his arms about the shaking body.

His lips formed a thin line as he considered Clyde's comment. How could anyone think he would assault his ward? Yet, feeling her in his arms, he knew he had to protect her.

His heartbeat quickened at her warmth. When had he developed a fondness for the girl? How had she managed to get through all his careful barriers? Yet she had. She was a part of him as Lizzy never had been.

"Deena," he said, only to be summarily interrupted as Helen swung into the room.

At the sight of Deena fast in Stern's arms, she sucked in a deep breath. "What's the meaning of this, young lady? I cannot believe the things Clyde said of you, why—"

"Enough!" thundered Stern, cowing Helen. "Surely Deena didn't invite that bounder to Three Oaks. I'm wondering who did?" His eyes narrowed speculatively.

Patting Deena's arm, Helen sat close to them. "Of course I wouldn't do such a thing, Kyle. Clyde seemed convinced Deena had invited him."

"Never!" Deena whispered desperately, looking up at Stern. "He frightens me. He hurt me."

"Helen, Clyde is not, under any circumstances, welcome at Three Oaks. There is to be no misunderstanding on this."

Helen soothed. "I had no idea. He was Lizzy's friend. I assumed—"

"Helen, I expect you to help me protect Deena."

"Of course we'll protect the dear child, even against her own foolishness. But Kyle, there's only one way to squelch rumors of her living here with you—marriage." She all but purred.

Thoughtfully, Stern looked down at Deena's bowed head. "Mayhap you're right, Helen. It seems a mite premature, but. . ."

He felt Deena tremble and wondered. "We must speak of this later, in private, Helen. First, I need to speak to Deena."

Smiling, Helen stood and gracefully walked from the room.

"Deena," he said, "what did Clyde do to you?"

Was not Lizzy's betrayal pain enough? He thought, at times, she went to Porter just out of spite. Porter would not come uninvited. Something did not set right. For all that, he found it impossible to lay blame on the young woman whose large eyes stared at him dazed with hurt and shock.

His heart thumped against his rib cage. No longer could he deny his feelings for his ward. She shared his faith, so important after Lizzy. She was also loving and caring, and Amy loved her.

Deena colored, hid her face against him. "Why did he want to hurt me?"

The ingenuousness of the cry melted the last of her guardian's reserve. "The man is a beast. I can only speculate he wished to hurt you for his own perverted pleasure. I meant to keep my promise to you. I had no idea he would dare come to Three Oaks."

Gently, he pulled her back into his arms, absently stroking the long, lovely hair, hair that wove itself into his dreams.

Warm and vibrant, Deena nestled against him. Over her head, Stern smiled.

He must do the right thing by Deena, young and vulnerable, but definitely not a child. "Deena." He waited until she lifted her tearstained face. "Would you like always to live at Three Oaks as part of my family?"

Pushing away, Deena tried to judge Stern's intentions. "Please, may I stay? I love Amy, and Three Oaks, and. . ."

"Go on."

Deena would have hid against him again, but Stern would not permit her to. "Look at me, Deena." Her eyes shyly met his. "I want you to finish your sentence. You love?"

"I cannot. You already think me a green goose. If you knew. . .I have no right." She bit her lip.

"Deena, it is vital I know." There was no gainsaying him.

Deena swallowed. "I lo. . .care for you." It came out barely above a whisper.

A chuckle rumbled from deep inside him. "Are you certain of your feelings?"

"I didn't want to, I just do." She brushed fresh tears from her cheeks.

"Shh. Don't be angry. I'm not laughing at you." Her confession warmed his heart. "As difficult as it may be to believe, Deena, I care very much for you. I want to give you a home. I want to protect you not only from beasts like Porter, but also from vicious gossip."

Deena looked away. "You'll marry Helen then."

Stern frowned at her assumption. "What?"

"Isn't that how you'll provide a stable home for me?" Her voice sounded bleak.

He smiled. "I shall take care of you, Lady Deena Heyford, but you must promise to trust me to do what is best. . .for all of us."

Reluctantly, Deena nodded.

nine

Once more, Deena found herself on the way to Portsmouth along with Amy and her guardian. Deena stared out the window, where at times the trees grew so thick and close to the road, branches slapped the side. An especially loud crack made Deena pale as she once more saw the tree crashing down on Princess.

It had been scarce a fortnight since the incidents with Princess and Porter. Deena shivered at the memory.

Somehow the indestructible little mare had managed to escape, on her own, with but minor cuts and bruises, which was why Stern returned home so much earlier than expected.

Helen was a puzzle. Deena fully expected an excited announcement of coming nuptials. It did not come.

Then came Stern's decision to return to Portsmouth. Twice, Deena tried to ask her guardian about Helen, only to have him pat her shoulder gently. "Be patient, Deena."

Deena thought of that now as she looked up into the bright sunlight. At noon, after spreading out a blanket under the trees, Stern eased himself down between Deena and Amy before opening the large, well-stocked basket.

Taking Amy's hand on one side, and Deena's on the other, Stern bowed his head. "Thank you, Lord, for this beautiful day and this bountiful feast You've provided. Protect us as we travel."

To her surprise, he squeezed her hand before releasing it. Deena's heart sang.

To Amy's delight, Deena passed out chicken, cold sliced venison, a loaf of warm brown bread with fresh butter and strawberry preserves. After downing the last of the blueberry tarts, they wiped their hands clean on the damp towel provided.

Hardly waiting for Stern to finish, Amy tackled her father,

who rolled backward, taking her with him. Stern's mask dropped away completely as he played with his daughter, chasing and being chased, much to Amy's delight.

Up in the trees birds twittered, leaves rustled. The sun shone down, the heat cooled by the gentle breeze. 'Twas an idyllic setting. . .if only. Deena looked away.

Stern plopped himself beside Deena. His long arm enfolded her. "Mustn't leave out the rest of our family, right, Amy?"

Laughing, Amy hugged her aunt. "Mustn't forget Auntie Deena," she agreed. The gesture warmed her lonely heart. As Deena returned Amy's hug, she glanced up at Stern and was disconcerted at the tenderness in his eyes.

⁂

Inside the house, Rhonda and James greeted them. "Welcome, Deena." Rhonda's ample arms enveloped her.

As Rhonda released her, Deena glanced past James to a young man with a thin face and smiling brown eyes. Medium of build, his hair stamped him as his father's son.

Stern drew Deena beside him. "Daniel, I'd like to make you acquainted to Deena Heyford."

They moved into the unusual family room with its mix of colors and style, where she sat next to her guardian on a velvet-covered couch. Conversation buzzed about her and she stifled a yawn.

To her embarrassment, conversation immediately ceased. "My dear, the trip has been wearing. Mayhap—" Rhonda was interrupted by the arrival of Saul and the young woman Deena recalled from her last visit. The lovely young woman's blond curls peeked out of her mobcap as she poured and handed out tea with all the graciousness of a hostess. Observing her long slender fingers and patrician features, Deena puzzled over the woman's place in this home.

After Saul and the girl left, Deena asked, "Who was that?"

Rhonda frowned. "The girl's name is Andrea. She came over to work for us."

"I see." But in truth Deena did not.

Daniel said, "Andrea agreed to work for us for five years in return for a new start in America." He glanced toward his mother. "Her time is soon up."

"Do many come over this way?"

"In the old days," said Rhonda, "many came over as indentured servants. They worked for a number of years then were given their own start.

If she had known, she would have done the same as Andrea.

Later, after she retired to her room, Rhonda asked, "Kyle, are you sure about this?"

"Quite sure," he said firmly.

Concern set her lips. "Does Helen know?"

"Helen's not my keeper." Stern set down his cup with a decided clink. Apologizing curtly, he strode from the room.

When Deena rang for a maid, she was pleasantly surprised when Andrea showed up to assist her. "My lady?"

Deena indicated the gown she wished to wear. As the taller girl slid the blue gown with its lace overdress from the wardrobe, she smoothed its silky folds.

Deena touched her arm. "Andrea, who are you?"

"Your maidservant, miss." Andrea sounded bleak.

"Andrea, you're wellborn. What happened?"

Andrea shrugged. "Six years past, Papa died."

"Go on."

"My second cousin Giles who inherited the earldom." She shuddered. "He was old, and cruel, and had every intention of making me his third wife. I–I ran away."

"Weren't there any relatives to whom you could turn?"

"The Earl of Liverpool is a connection."

"The Prime Minister? Surely. . ."

Andrea shook her head. "They're friends. I was afraid."

"So you came to America to work as a servant."

" 'Tis better, a thousand times better, than being married to that debauched roué!"

"Now there is Daniel."

Andrea stared at her. "How did you—? It matters not. Mrs. Bates won't allow her son to be matched with one of their own serving maids."

"And Daniel. Does he hold you in tender affection?"

"In truth we have pledged ourselves secretly. He approached his mother, but she's afraid of a scandal like that which erupted before the war for independence."

"Here I thought my sister was the biggest scandal of the family. But what other scandal was this?"

"Scandal in some minds." Andrea folded her hands. "You know how the ton gossips. Well, 'tis not so different here. Seems a relative, one of the state's great governors, married his young maidservant some years after the death of his wife. She was of good family, lively, intelligent. Made no difference. Society shunned her. Daniel told me they said things like 'she's just an ambitious hussy.' Nothing changes."

Andrea tugged the edge of her apron. "Mrs. Bates fears marrying a servant will affect Daniel's ministry prospects." She choked back a sob. "I love him so."

"Daniel?"

"Too honorable to go against the wishes of his family." Andrea sighed; her shoulders slumped.

"I thought things were different here."

≈

When Deena entered the anteroom, her eyes flashed with determination. Stern, seeing the look, sighed and took her hand. "You're late."

"I'm sorry." She glanced toward Daniel.

"Deena, glad you're here. If Jonathan were here, our circle would be complete."

What about Andrea? Deena questioned silently. The whole of it seemed vastly unfair. They included her, why not Andrea?

After the usual delicious dinner, the men walked with the ladies back to the family room. As she sat next to Stern, the door opened and the three cousins ran in. Amy flung herself into her father's arms.

He scolded gently. "Amy, you must learn decorum."

Amy wrinkled her nose. "Papa, I'd never get nowhere then."

"Anywhere," Deena corrected automatically.

"I'd get no anywhere," Amy corrected herself. Stern

chuckled at the chagrin on Deena's face.

The exchange was lost in Amy's effusive hugs. "Night, Papa. Night, Auntie Deena." She wished the others good night, then, with her more decorous cousins, left for the upstairs nursery and bed.

Daniel laughed. "Growing up fast, Uncle. Going to be a charmer, that one."

Stern's face darkened. "She's a good child. I'll see she becomes a godly woman."

Daniel cleared his throat. "I meant nothing amiss, Uncle."

Rhonda broke the tense silence. "High time the girl has a mother."

"Rhonda." Stern sounded a warning. He turned to his ward. "Deena, be ready by nine," he said abruptly. "I'm taking you and Amy to be fitted."

"But—" she thought of her extensive wardrobe.

Stern's expression softened at her confusion. "These are rather special gowns."

The conversation turned to the business of shipping. Deena listened to the fascinating details of shipping along the Piscataqua from the forming of the tall pine masts to the launching of the ship itself.

It was not until Rhonda rang for coffee and chocolate after ten that Deena thought again of Andrea's problem. As though her thoughts conjured her up, Andrea entered, pushing a wheeled cart. Eyes averted, she picked the tray from the cart and set it on the low table in front of Rhonda.

Deena watched Daniel. As Andrea entered, his lips tightened. His gaze never left Andrea's graceful form. Briefly, she caught his eye. Something akin to embarrassment crossed his face.

"That will be all," Rhonda brusquely dismissed the girl.

"Yes, ma'am." Andrea fled.

"Daniel," Rhonda chided, "you must not encourage the girl. She has her place. Not for you, Daniel."

"Mother, this is not the time."

"We're all family, Daniel. Deena, of course, doesn't know." Rhonda smiled distantly.

"But I do." Deena's eyes flashed. "I talked to Andrea."

"Make no mistake," said Rhonda, "she's out for the main chance, and I'll not have my son ensnared."

Deena turned to Daniel, who sat stiffly in his chair, his cheek muscle twitching nervously. "Your son has done the compromising, not Andrea."

The warning in Stern's eyes didn't stop her. "Have you considered that mayhap Daniel and Andrea truly care for each other?"

"Passing fancy," James tried to defuse the tension.

Deena stared at Daniel's flushed face. "Is that all it is? And you claim the sanctity of a minister's garb. Andrea certainly believes elsewhere."

Rhonda puffed up angrily. "How dare you accuse my son of impropriety! Look to your own house, miss. Your sister was the master of deception."

Deena's anger melted under the onslaught.

Daniel shifted, his face pale. "Deena, I—" He gulped, raised his hand to still his mother's protestations.

"Deena speaks the truth. I, indeed, have been dishonest in my attentions to Andrea. Mother, Father I have been dishonest with you as well. Most of all, I have not been honest with myself. I told Andrea I needed your blessing for our union."

"What!" Rhonda slumped against the cushions.

"I had hoped, in time, you would accustom yourself to the situation." He leaned forward, hands clasped with new purpose. "Mother, Andrea and I have pledged ourselves to each other. I love her. With or without your approval, I plan on taking Andrea as my wife." He smiled then at Deena. "Thank you for speaking the truth as I have not." He nodded toward Kyle. "This one is wise beyond her years, Uncle."

Rhonda sputtered, having lost steam in the face of Daniel's confession. "You have no notion of her background, her family."

"It matters not, Mother. She's above reproach. And I love her."

Rhonda gulped. James looked at his son with new respect.

"Are you certain, Son?"

"I am, Father."

"Then you have our blessing." He quelled Rhonda's protests. "That's right, my dear, our blessing."

"The scandal," whispered Rhonda.

Stern broke. "You're concerned about scandal after Lizzy?"

"Listen," said Deena. "Andrea's father was the Earl of Wattenshire."

Rhonda all but snorted. "And what reason did she give for running away?"

"Check Debretts," Deena said. "A confirmed rake inherited the title. As her guardian, he intended to force Andrea into marriage, though he was much older."

She felt Stern tense.

Daniel recovered first. "There you are, Mother. It seems it's not a matter of whether she's good enough for me, but whether or not I'm worthy of her."

Rhonda capitulated completely. "Obviously cultured, well-mannered. Yes, umm." Deena could almost see Rhonda's mind marshaling her thoughts.

"First thing, relieve her of all duties. Let it out about her background."

James patted his wife's arm. "Romantics will love the story, Rhonda."

"So much to plan. The wedding next year."

"No, Mother, I have dallied with Andrea long enough. Six months at the latest."

Sighing, Rhonda nodded. "Going to be a busy summer, weddings, weddings, weddings."

James winked at Deena.

Daniel leaned forward, took her hand. "Thank you, Deena. Remember, no matter what, you'll always have two friends . . .Andrea and I."

Deena did not know how soon those words would echo in her mind.

ten

The next morning, Stern appeared distracted as he escorted Amy and Deena to the dressmaker's.

From the next booth, Deena heard Amy's delighted squeal as the new gown rustled down around her. Smiling, Deena stood quietly as the dressmaker fastened the myriad of pearl buttons down the back of the fine Italian silk gown. The shoulders puffed becomingly, adding width to her shoulders. The molded bodice with its heart-shaped neckline showed off her young curves. A gossamer, silvery lace overdress floated out from the fine silk skirt. The whole moved deliciously against her skin.

Staring into the mirror against the far wall, she could scarce take in the transformation. The gown perfectly set off her pale skin and silver hair.

"You're a fairy princess," breathed Amy.

"And your dress is perfect for you." The gown was off-white to better go with Amy's golden hair.

Laughing, she cried, "Come on, let's show Papa!"

The dressmaker protested. "No. Mr. Stern specifically requested not to see the gowns."

A few moments later the modiste spoke to Stern. "The gowns need little altering. I'll have them sent this afternoon, if that meets with your approval." Stern nodded.

As they left in the carriage, Amy complained. "Papa, she wouldn't let us show you our pretty dresses. We looked *sooo* beautiful, especially Auntie Deena."

Stern chuckled. "I promise you, I'll see them soon." With that, he changed the subject.

Deena felt a reserve toward her. Of course, he was still angry about her rudeness the evening before, even if it was for a good cause. Deena could not blame him. Surely she might have dealt with the problem without being rude.

It did not then surprise her overmuch when, on arriving at the Bates's house, Stern led her off to a sitting room.

Handing her into a chairback settee, Stern sat down heavily beside her. Deena tensed. "About last night. I apologize, Mr. Stern. I'm sorry for embarrassing you in front of your family."

Stern surveyed his tense ward. To her amazement, he gently slipped an arm about her rigid shoulders.

"I'm not angry at you, Deena. Despite your temper, you did confront a situation which needed attention."

"I don't understand. Rhonda always seemed so caring, why would she dismiss Andrea as she did?"

Absently, Stern tugged a lock of her hair. "Rhonda has had more than her share of dealing with family scandals. She suffered much humiliation at Lizzy's hands. She did not wish to face the possibility of another."

"I'm so sorry." Tears filled Deena's eyes.

Stern's expression softened. "You've done nothing amiss."

When Deena looked up, Stern lost himself in her deep eyes. "Do you consider me old?"

"Oh, no, Mr. Stern. You're a fine figure of a man." She blushed furiously.

Some of the tension faded from Stern's face. "Would you truly like to belong to me, to be my family?"

"Yes." Deena bit her lip, wondering where this conversation was leading. "Is Helen to become mistress of Three Oaks?"

"No indeed. She's but a dear friend." He shook his head as though to clear away painful memories.

Love for him radiated from her face to his heart. Guilt ate at him. Did she know that even now, he found it hard to trust her completely? Yet, she touched something deep inside him. Was it his youth, his ideals. . .or his faith?

"Ah, my dear Deena. I am plagued to the death with this Mr. Stern this, and Mr. Stern that. I'd like you to address me as Kyle." He cupped her chin in his large hand.

"K–Kyle," Deena stuttered.

He chuckled at her utter confusion as he brushed her lips with a kiss.

۶

The next morning, the maids were in a flurry about Deena, dressing her in her new white gown. Andrea, herself, buttoned the myriad of buttons.

"Are you certain Mr. Stern wishes me to wear this gown this morning?" The young maids giggled. Andrea finally waved them from the room.

"No mistake, Miss Heyford."

"Deena, please call me Deena. After all, we'll soon be a close connection."

Taking care not to crush the gown, Andrea hugged her. "Daniel told me how brave you were. He was so upset about how he'd treated me." She blushed prettily. "And Mrs. Bates I mean Rhonda, bustled about acting for all the world as though the whole of it was her idea. That woman does love to organize. Daniel and I are of a mind to leave all that to her."

Running in, Amy twirled about in her new gown. "I'm so beautiful. Everyone says so." She stopped suddenly, awed. "Oh, Auntie Deena. You're most beautiful of all."

Amy stared up at Andrea. "I'm glad Daniel is marrying you."

Andrea blushed. Firmly taking the little girl's hand, she led her from the room. "How about helping me dress?"

She glanced back. "Mr. Stern says to wait for him."

Impatiently, Deena awaited her guardian. Surely it was far too early for a formal party. An assembly? Did it matter? She knew she could scarcely wait to see Kyle again.

Kyle eyes showed his appreciation of the lovely picture she made. "Are you ready, dear?" He took her arm, steadying his voice as he gazed at the confection of silk and lace, feeling his whole body respond to her as a man. His chest tightened. Mayhap his plan would be more difficult to adhere to than he first believed.

Lord am I doing the right thing? I thought this came from You, and yet. . .

He held out a small box. "Thank you," Deena responded automatically, then gasped when she found a diamond necklace nestled on a black velvet interior. "For me!"

She trembled as her guardian placed them about her neck.

He smiled down at her tenderly. "Come," he said.

With infinite care, he handed Deena into a newly painted white and gold carriage before sitting down beside her.

"What about Amy?"

"Ah," he smiled down at her, "she and the others have gone on ahead."

Deena lowered her eyes from the intensity of his gaze. He squeezed her hand. "You do trust me?"

She glanced up into his anxious face. What was she to say? Silence reigned as the coach moved through the streets to stop in front of an impressive Federal-style white church.

Surprisingly, Kyle made no effort to disembark. "Deena," he tightened his grip on her hand.

Sparks of fear ignited inside her. "What is it?"

"Deena," he said again, carefully watching her face, "I brought you here to make you my wife."

Deena's mouth dropped open. Her eyes widened in shock. She could not speak. Stern continued. "Deena, I've come to care for you. And Amy needs a mother."

Misinterpreting her shocked silence, Stern sighed. "I'm sorry, Deena. This comes as too much of a shock. Rhonda said I was foolish to spring this on you like this, but after what you said. . .how you felt." His vulnerability touched her. "Never mind. I understand."

Deena held the arm that reached to summon the coachman. "Mr. Stern. Kyle. Wish you truly to marry *me?*"

"Most certainly." He looked deep into her bewildered eyes. "Will you do me the honor of becoming my wife?"

"Yes, Kyle. I would be most honored."

Fumbling for his handkerchief, Stern wiped the tears from her cheeks. Laughter twinkled in his eyes. "Mustn't spill over like a beanpot too long over the fire."

Deena giggled. "What?"

"An old saying. I feared I offended you beyond recall."

At the front of the church, Andrea, in a rose and silver gown, awaited her along with an excited Amy, tightly holding a basket of flowers. On the other side Daniel stood with Kyle, both resplendent in black cutaways.

As organ music echoed throughout the building, Rhonda hugged her. "God bless you."

James stepped up then. Proudly taking her arm in his, he led her down the aisle. Once she stumbled, but James held her firmly and they continued. Embarrassed, her eyes sought those of her bridegroom. Did her awkwardness disgust him? No, there was nothing but tenderness in his eyes.

She noticed his once carefully folded kerchief hanging limply from his pocket. Her heart ached for this giant of a man who had planned this wonderful surprise for her.

Solemnly they exchanged vows—hers soft, Kyle's firm.

As Deena leaned on Stern's arm, the black-robed minister intoned seriously, "Husbands, love your wives, even as Christ also loved the church, and gave himself for it. . .

"Nevertheless let every one of you in particular so love his wife even as himself; and the wife see that she reverence her husband." The minister flipped the pages of his large Bible and continued reading.

Closing the book, the minister solemnly gave the references, "From Ephesians 5." For the next ten minutes he expounded on the verses. Deena scarcely heard him.

She stared down at the ring sparkling on her finger. It was a beautiful ring of fine diamonds set on a thin silver band. Thoughtfully, Kyle had a matching ring made for himself, which she set on his finger with a hand that so trembled her new husband had to help her.

Almost before she knew it, Stern had her back into the carriage and headed back to the Bates's house. Deena walked into the dining room on Stern's arm as though walking in a dream.

The room was festooned with streamers. Red and white roses decorated every available space. Fine china and silverware caught the streams of sunlight flooding through the open windows. They sparkled no brighter than Deena's face.

Amy tugged at her skirt. Seeing the girl's serious face, she leaned down. "Yes?"

"Auntie Deena, are you my mama now?"

Smiling, Kyle squatted to Amy's level. "Do you want her to be your mother?"

"Oh, yes, Papa."

"Then you may address her as such."

She hugged her father. "Thank you, Papa. Thank you." Looking up at her aunt, she whispered, "Mama." Then more firmly. "Mama."

Deena hugged the little girl. "I love you, Amy. I'm proud to have you as my daughter." Amy beamed.

Deena's happiness stayed with her as she dozed against Stern's shoulder on the long ride back to Three Oaks. Was it a dream she felt him stroke her hair? Rousing slightly, she gazed up into his face, soft with tenderness.

"You have such lovely hair, dearest Deena."

"Swedish ancestors," she murmured drowsily.

"And are you happy?"

"La. Never did I think. . .consider. . .that you might want me." She fell silent, realizing suddenly her new husband had said naught of love. . .protection for her, mother for Amy, but not love. Studying Kyle's strong face, she knew she loved him. But would her love be enough?

After the couple received the congratulations of the retainers in the large hall, Mrs. Cairns took Amy off to bed. At the doorway, Amy turned and with a smug look on her face declared, "Now Mrs. Billings can't never be my mother."

Mrs. Cairns hustled the little girl away before her father opened his mouth. Even as he led Deena from the room, a frown settled on his lips. Stealing a glance at Stern's face, she knew Amy had conjured up a specter that distanced her from her new husband.

eleven

With a minute creak, the door opened and Kyle, dressed in a white-frogged blue robe, stood beside the bed.

Stern's breath caught in his throat at the picture Deena made in her white gown with her hair spilling over her shoulders. Forcing a smile, Stern sat down on the edge of the bed, facing her. Taking Deena's cold hands in his, he rubbed warmth back into them.

He ached to hold her in his arms. Ached to make her his. But she was vulnerable, and he must not frighten her as did Clyde. Though something inside warned otherwise, he'd set his mind to gain her trust slowly.

"Deena, my dear."

Deena blushed.

"Deena, this has been a very special day in our lives. One I pray you shall never regret."

Stern misinterpreted the hesitation in her eyes. "Deena, this is all new to you and I don't want to do anything to frighten you. I would have waited but for the rumors, and the need to give you more protection than I felt I could give as your guardian."

"Oh." Deena winced. "Is that the only reason you married me?"

Kyle stared at her, nonplused.

Tugging her hand from his grasp, she continued. "I cannot fathom how your sister would sanction me as your wife, yet reject Andrea for Daniel."

Sitting back, Kyle studied his wife. "Rhonda preferred you . . .anyone, in truth, to Helen, whom she mistakenly assumed would one day finagle me to the altar."

"Your sister disapproves of Helen?"

Kyle glanced away. "She didn't feel Helen's past stood up

to scrutiny. Helen did some inadvisable things when she was quite young. When she married, she became the model of respectability—far more so, I might add, than Lizzy."

"So you never truly wished me to wife," Deena whispered.

Gently, Kyle turned her face to his and flinched at the hurt he saw reflected in her deep gray eyes. "After Lizzy, I determined never again to marry, because I didn't wish to open myself to that kind of pain. . .not again."

Seeing Deena's eyes soften, Stern stroked her cheek. "Then you came with your living faith and compassionate heart, and down went all my presumptions. You've become very special."

Leaning forward, Deena interrupted. "Did you marry me just to quell the rumors?"

"No indeed." Gently, Kyle slipped an arm about Deena. "Deena, I don't wish to frighten you like Clyde did. Because of that and your youth, I've decided to wait to. . .to share the same bed."

Deena pulled away. "You don't want me. Is it because of my bad leg?"

"Nonsense! That's the least of my concerns. I want to give you time to get over the shock of what Clyde attempted to do, time to grow up."

Smiling timidly, she touched his anxious face. "You labor under a misconception of my age. I am indeed old enough to take to wife."

Kyle kissed her cheek. "I know what you're about and it will not signify, Deena." He placed a finger over her parted lips. "No use protesting. You have some growing up to do before we broach this subject again."

He sighed as she tried to hide her hurt. "Whatever your age, Deena, you're already adjusting to having an older daughter and managing a household."

Before she could reply, Stern leaned over and kissed her sweet lips. She would never know how much it pained him to leave her alone in the large bed on the night of their wedding.

Tears coursed down Deena's cheeks as she buried her head

in her pillow to muffle her painful sobs. She felt bereft, alone. 'Twas a long time before sleep came, but long before it did the aching pain inside knotted. "Jesus, I love him so. I thought maybe he loved me, too, but he doesn't. He married me simply for the sake of appearance. Oh, Jesus, what will I do?"

Be his friend, she heard. *He needs you, but he's been hurt and is afraid.*

"But Lord."

Be his friend.

Be his friend? Closing her eyes, she let go her hurt. "All right, Jesus. I'll be his friend."

Good.

Deena awoke in the lovely room feeling strange, as though she didn't belong. Mayhap her bedchamber seemed strange, but Three Oaks itself welcomed her. She, not Helen, was mistress here. It was a heady consideration.

Deena dreaded meeting up with Helen until Enid informed her (with obvious glee), "Mrs. Billings be gone ta visit friends. Says she'll be gone a few days, mayhap longer."

At that moment the door banged open and Amy ran in to embrace her.

"Whoa, Amy, you'll knock me over!" Deena drew back at the little girl's exuberance.

"Oh, Mama, I don't ever want to hurt you." She hugged Deena more gently.

"I know, dear," Deena returned her hug. "Now, what's so important?"

"Papa says he hired a man to paint us." She skipped around the room, coming full circle to stand beside her mother. "We get to get all dressed up in our new dresses and get painted."

"Truly!"

Amy beheld her new mother with impatience. "Of course, Mama. Papa's gonna hang it in," momentarily her voice caught, "in place of my mama's, my other mama's picture."

Deena knew how much the portrait of Beth meant to the little girl. "But—"

"Papa said you're my mama now. He's right, you know."

Amy sounded very grown up. " 'Sides, Papa said he'll put my other mama's picture where I can look at it when I want to." Again she danced about.

"Just think. We're getting painted, you and me together."

"You and I," Deena corrected. "That will be pretty special."

The little girl's hug threatened to undo the careful chignon at the base of Deena's neck. As Amy danced out of the chamber, she turned back to deliver a message. "Papa wants to see you in his study."

Hesitantly, Deena knocked at the study door. "You sent for me?" She sounded like a housekeeper. "If I interrupted—"

"You're welcome anytime, Deena." He surveyed her morning gown with approval. "Sleep well?"

Deena colored, nodding diffidently. Kyle seemed not to notice her hesitancy as he seated her on a settee.

He glanced at the gold-cased watch hanging from a chain on his waistcoat. "Still have some time before luncheon." Tucking the watch back into his blue waistcoat, he sat next to his wife, stretching out a long arm behind her shoulders. Deena stiffened.

Frowning, Stern removed his arm. "I know I should have waited. Especially since this is supposed to be our honeymoon." Deena stared down at her clenched hands, determined to just be friends.

More gently this time, Stern's arm encircled her shoulders and drew her to him. "Deena. Please look at me." His uncertainty softened her. She looked up.

"Thank you," he said, giving her a quick hug. "I hope you won't be angry about this. . .Mr. Debussy."

Deena smiled then, "The artist? Amy told me."

"Upset?"

"No."

"I just thought. . .well, never mind. I wanted your portrait. . . and Amy's. You looked so lovely in your wedding gown." He tucked an errant curl behind her ear. "Lovely. . .very lovely." His lips were just inches from her own.

Deena closed her eyes; her throat tightened at his nearness.

His lips brushed her hair. She tried to still the disappointment coursing through her.

Later that afternoon, Deena sat in the parlor writing at the secretariat. Sighing, Deena picked up the quill pen and began to write.

> *Dear Margaret and Orrin,*
> *You will not conceive what has transpired. . . .*

Careful not to reveal the true state of her marriage, Deena wrote them of her new life. Trying to decide how best to continue without making them suspicious, Deena tapped the quill on the writing mat, dulling the tip. Absently sharpening it with the small silver knife, she continued writing, couching her request casually:

> *Rumor has it I am much too young for Mr. Stern.*
> *Speaking plainly, it would be of great assistance if Orrin*
> *might provide me with proof of my birth year. 'Twould*
> *do much to quell the rumors.*

Quickly finishing the letter, Deena handed the letter over to Bailey to mail.

As she started up the stairs, the butler admitted a short, balding gentleman who expressed himself through his hands, small hands with long slender fingers.

Deena met him in the entry hall. "Mr. Debussy."

The man's smile widened as his eyes swept over her. "My lady." He kissed her hand. "At your service, mon ami. Please tell me it is you I have come to paint." His words were heavily accented, his eyes lingering with delight on Deena's hair. "Perfection," he breathed.

Deena took the Frenchman's exaggerated compliments lightly. "Yes, my husband wishes my portrait and that of his daughter."

"You, then, are the mistress of the house." He bowed again as, blushing, Deena acknowledged her status. "Ah, a bride. It weel pleasure me to paint such a one."

Though she tried not to show it, Deena was almost as excited as Amy over the portrait, over the thought Kyle wanted one of her. They watched as Jacques created a studio with just the right sunlight for his work.

Over and over he posed her in the rose-covered chair with Amy at her side. To Amy's constant frustration, he would not even begin until everything was perfect.

The artist exulted over Deena's hair. "Merveilleux, glorieux. . .wondrous, glorious," until Deena felt uncomfortable.

He insisted she leave it cascading over her shoulders. Kyle heartily agreed.

"It makes me feel uncomfortable," Deena told Kyle that night as he sat on the edge of her bed. Deena had come to covet this time of intimacy.

Stern stroked her hair, " 'Tis far too lovely to hide."

Deena smiled at him, love in her eyes. Her days often seemed but a prelude to these nighttime tête-à-têtes which grew from minutes to an hour or more as they shared with each other. During these times, as their hearts bonded into friendship, Deena began to understand the deep hurt Kyle had suffered, came to understand as well his deep faith.

Despite her sister's perfidy, in some strange way, she sensed Kyle still blamed himself for the ultimate failure of the marriage, still found it difficult to trust.

Often he held her hand, stroked her cheek or hair. He was gentle and tender with her. While Deena ached for more, ached for his arms to hold her tight, ached to know she truly mattered to this husband, she feared that if she shared her heart, he would reject her.

Stern, too, coveted this time with the woman he was coming to appreciate more each day. He delighted in her quick, practical mind, her compassionate nature.

Mornings he enjoyed riding with her, enjoyed watching the unabashed joy and wonder on her face. How could he not know how lonely he had become or how much he craved having someone to share not just his life, but also the things that mattered most to him? Deena, dear Deena, believed as he believed, had similar tastes in music and art and books and. . . the list went on and on.

Then there was their shared faith.

The nearest church was a far pace and open only sporadically whenever a minister was in the area. This was the Sunday.

Amy bounced up and down on the hard seat of the chaise where she sat between Deena and her father. "Oh, oh. This is fun, Auntie, I mean, Mama."

Deena exchanged an amused smile with Kyle before addressing the girl. " 'Tis indeed, Amy. But dearest, you must try to sit still or you'll wrinkle your muslin beyond recall." Reaching over, Deena tugged Amy's bonnet further forward on the girl's head.

Amy sat still for a minute, mayhap two, then, bubbling over with excitement, she turned and waved to Esie and her family directly behind them in the procession from Three Oaks. "This is more fun than sitting in the parlor." Amy wrinkled her nose.

Deena glanced quickly at her husband. She, herself, rather enjoyed Sunday mornings when Stern gathered family and staff together for a short time of meditation and Bible reading and prayer.

Today was the first time Deena would be actually attending a church service since arriving in America. Her stomach fluttered. Would she be accepted as Stern's bride? The eight miles along the rutted road only increased her anxiety.

Overhead, the sun shone down from a clear blue sky. Amy wiggled in her seat, then stilled at her father's frown. But for Deena's anxious thoughts, it would have been the perfect day for an outing.

Quietly, Stern quoted Psalm 118:24: "This is the day which the Lord hath made; we will rejoice and be glad in it." Smiling down at Deena, he said, "Everything will be fine." She nodded.

He had all but heaved a sigh of relief when she came downstairs earlier dressed in her dove gray gown trimmed in white, as though he expected to find her inappropriately gowned.

Lizzy, of course, would have dressed to shock. She would have to prove to Stern she was not Lizzy. . .not in any way.

Though they had an early start, by the time they arrived at the white clapboard Congregational church, the yard was already filled with an assortment of carriages, buckboards, and other vehicles. Some were new or newly painted, others were worn with age.

Skillfully, Kyle edged the curricle as close as possible to the door of the church. Hopping down, he secured the team before turning to assist Amy and Deena. Excitedly, Amy scrambled down before he could grab for her.

"Amy," Deena chided, "you must learn to await assistance. You might have torn your gown."

The little girl hung her head. "Sorry." She waited quietly while Stern lifted Deena down beside her. He looked down at his daughter.

"I expect you to conduct yourself like a lady. You will, at all times, obey your mother. Is that clear?" In his somber black, he reminded Deena of an Old Testament prophet.

Amy gulped. "Yes, Papa."

As Deena took Kyle's proffered arm, she murmured, "Do not be overly hard on her, Kyle."

Stern's lips twitched. Patting Deena's hand he whispered, "I'll try, my dear. Are you all right?"

Deena thrilled at his concern. She leaned heavily on his arm, wishing she had opportunity to massage her leg after the long ride. "I think so."

Inside the church, Deena's heart sank. The building was nearly full, but at Stern's insistence the usher found her and Amy a place on one of the hard, narrow pews. Kyle himself and most of the others stood at the rear of the building. Deena felt uncomfortable among the small congregation that consisted of small farmers, laborers, and a few large landowners.

She tried to concentrate on the long service, but Amy wriggled as the black-robed minister droned on. Though Deena enjoyed the sermon, she recalled how long Sunday mornings could be for a child.

Did Amy also sense the cold stares, the tension? Unfortunately, the end of the service but signaled the beginning of an afternoon of socializing.

The congregation filed out quietly, then friends drifted together, chatting, laughing. Stern took Deena's arm and walked with her to the carriage, where he pulled out an enormous picnic basket.

She watched the men set up makeshift tables, then drift to one side away from the women busily spreading out the feast. Under the wide trees, Amy giggled with other girls her age.

"Feelin' out ta place, ma'am?" Esie patted Deena's arm. "Don't think I didn't see those biddies lookin' down their noses at you."

Gratefully, Deena followed Esie to the long tables. Esie boldly made way for them among the crowd of women chatting gaily as they set out roast, boiled, salted, and fried pork, beef, ham, venison, turkey. There was loaf after loaf of wheat, rye, barley, and other breads. There were thick brown beans in deep pots. Desserts filled one end of the table. Deena smiled, thinking of Amy's delight.

"Mrs. Stern, Mrs. Thomas and Mrs. Wright," Elsie said.

The two women hesitated, then acknowledged her reluctantly.

For a time, as Deena helped prepare the meal, she felt a growing acceptance. That ended abruptly when a plump woman in a well-cut but prim dress of dull brown accosted her.

"Be it true you're the sister of your husband's late wife?" She made it sound like an insult.

Deena gulped, but held the woman's gaze steadily. "I am."

"Just like her, too, is my guess." She raised an eyebrow at the women gathered around her. "You'd think the poor man would learn. 'Course there's always Mrs. Billings."

Several women gasped at the woman's ill manners. Others edged away from Deena as though she were somehow contaminated. Tears stung Deena's eyes and she lowered her head, hoping the others would not see.

Esie placed a protective arm about her. "Come, Deena. No need to stay with those with no manners." Determinedly she steered the numb Deena to Kyle, who stood slightly apart from the other men, listening.

He wrapped a long arm about her. "What happened?" He addressed Esie.

As Esie told him, in no uncertain terms, Deena drew on Stern's strength. She felt his body tense, sensed his anger. When Esie left them, he leaned down. "Would you like to go home, darling?"

Darling! He called her darling! Deena drowned in the tenderness she witnessed in his eyes. Oh, yes, she'd like to leave. The nerve of these Americans, judging her without even knowing her!

Beyond Kyle, Amy happily played with friends. Was not often she had such an opportunity and, from the looks of things, she was making the most of that opportunity. Lifting her head with new determination, Deena said, "No. I'll be fine."

"That's the spirit," he murmured. Deena basked in his warmth.

Nearby, the other men frowned at Stern's display of affection. With sudden revelation, Deena understood why Kyle had been standing apart even when she first came to him. He was no more accepted than she. Her need for attention hadn't made it any easier for him.

Pushing away, Deena stuttered, "I–I'll rejoin the ladies now." She glanced toward the men.

Kyle dropped his comforting hold. Deena's sensitivity amazed him once again. He watched her walk back toward the enclave of women, head high, shoulders back. Not a shred of her hurt showed on her carefully schooled features. There indeed was a lady to be proud of.

Lord, thank You for Deena. . .my wife. A smile spread across his face.

twelve

Though the afternoon sapped Deena's strength, she managed to get through the endless socializing with dignity. On the way home, with Amy sleeping against her arm, Deena felt Stern's arm drawing her to his shoulder.

"You did me proud," he said softly.

Deena gazed up at her husband, tears in her eyes. For the first time she felt part of him. Things would work out. All they needed was time, time alone, time to build a solid relationship. Deena couldn't help but wonder how Helen would take the news. Would she think her new friend had betrayed her?

Lord, I love my husband, she prayed silently. *He's my best friend, but I want more than friendship. Help Kyle learn to trust again.*

The very next day, Helen swept into the library.

Deena tensed as Stern put an arm around her shoulders. "Have you heard the news?"

" 'Tis true then." From the tautness of Helen's lips, Deena understood Helen's light tone dearly cost the woman.

"Indeed, if you heard Deena is now my wife. You said yourself, 'twas most unseemly for a young innocent to live unchaperoned in a bachelor establishment."

Helen's laugh was forced. "I had no idea you held such affection for your ward. Who is scarcely more than a child."

Deena gasped, "But Helen, you know how old I am."

"Age really isn't all that much of an issue, Helen. What does matter is that Deena is old enough to marry, and I'm glad God brought her into my life." Stern smiled down at her. "No one can cast aspersions on her now."

Deena warmed in his smile.

"Papa! Papa! Look what I have!" Amy skidded into the room. She cradled a scruffy looking gray and white cat.

"A cat!" Helen recoiled.

Amy's arms tightened, causing the cat to squirm. "Mama, may I keep this kitty?"

"Get that thing out of here!" choked Helen.

Amy backed up behind her mother. Automatically, Deena placed a protective arm around the girl.

Helen grabbed Stern's arm. "You know cats terrify me!"

"Helen, get ahold of yourself," Stern told her firmly. "You were a mere child when that rabid cat came after you. But this is only a tiny kitten."

"Amy, where did the cat come from?"

"Mrs. Cairns showed me. Cook brought the cats in to get a mouse in the kitchen. Please, Papa. Can't I have this one?" She snuggled the gray cat to her breast.

Kyle glanced at Deena. "What do you say?"

"Kyle," insisted Helen, "I'm sorry, but cats still terrify me. I won't have them around."

"Helen, I can understand your fear, but it does not signify here. I promise you the cat will not be taken to your house."

Deena petted the cat. "Where does Cook keep the cats?"

"She has a place fer them, Mama. Even a place to. . .well. . . you know. Sometimes she just lets them outside."

Looking from the cat's wide, languid eyes to Amy's, wide with pleading, Deena capitulated. "It appears the cats are needed. I see no reason why you can't keep this one as a pet."

Glancing up, she saw fear in Helen's eyes, and, just for a moment, anger. "Amy," she cautioned, "you must also keep the cat away from Mrs. Billings."

"Yes, Mama. Thank you, Mama." Cat still in her arms, Amy reached to hug her mother before bouncing from the room.

Helen's protest died in her throat at Kyle's tender smile toward Deena. "See, Helen. She's most capable."

"Kyle." She sidled closer to him. "There is still so much little Deena needs to learn."

Though Deena felt sorry for the woman, she wished Helen would spend less time at Three Oaks. But how could she convey this to Helen without hurting her feelings, especially since Kyle didn't seem to see the problem?

Fact is, Helen was, if anything, more in evidence than ever.

While Deena and Amy spent long hours posing for Debussy, Helen tried to help, imposing herself into almost everything, leaving Esie frustrated.

Then conflict began over Gray Lady, the little cat. Deena knew Amy did everything possible to stay out of Helen's way, but it seemed they all too often ended up in the same room. The inevitable result was Helen became frightened, then angry. Amy grew sullen. Was it all mere coincidence?

It happened again. Deena heard Helen's cry. "That cat again. I swear you deliberately try to scare me, young lady!"

Seeing Stern head for the door, Deena followed. "Helen, did you want me?"

"Kyle, I'm sorry, but it's that cat. I can't handle it."

Glancing at Kyle, she saw mistrust in his eyes. "Deena, what do you know about this?"

"Amy was playing with her cat," she informed him before addressing Helen. "Amy had no notion you were about."

"I'm so frightened of cats. I can't help it." She leaned weakly against Kyle, whose arm circled her absently.

"Amy," her father remonstrated, "you know better than to frighten Mrs. Billings."

"But, Papa!"

"I'll not have it, Amy, not if you want to keep that cat."

"No!" grabbing her cat, Amy ran from the room crying. "It's all her fault. Why doesn't she go home!"

"Deena, I'll not have my daughter act like that."

"I'll talk to her." Quelling her frustration with Helen, Deena quietly left to see to Amy.

After praying about it, Deena confronted Helen. "Helen, I'm sorry about your fear, but having a cat is good for Amy, especially since she hasn't any friends her age about. You can understand." Biting her lip, she prayed for the right words. "Now that Kyle and I are married. . . I thought, perhaps, you might wish to spend less time at Three Oaks."

Helen clenched her hands together. "I thought you were

such an innocent, but you snared him right from under me."

"Helen! He asked me to marry him, and I said yes. I'm sorry if you think I did it to hurt you. I didn't."

"You're just like Lizzy!" Helen condemned as she swept passed Deena with such force, Deena was thrown back against the sofa. Watching the woman leave, Deena shivered.

❧

"Helen, you wished to speak to me?" Entering the rose salon, Kyle glanced up toward Lizzy's picture and frowned. "I'll soon be moving that to a much less visible room. Debussy is making good progress on his painting, or so he tells me, since he won't permit anyone to view it until it's completed.

"I plan to hang the painting here. I plan on holding a reception to celebrate. What do you think?"

Patting the place beside her, Helen said, "Sounds fine, but. . ."

Kyle hesitated, then sat opposite in a large armchair. Helen frowned. "What is it, Helen?"

"I mislike bringing this up."

"Out with it, Helen. The cat again?"

"I hate to mention this, but. . .you know how Lizzy was."

Disbelief showed on Stern's face. "Surely you're not implying little Deena is taking after her sister."

Helen backed. "No, I guess not, though I did wonder about Clyde. I was speaking of Lizzy. Toward the end, she seemed unstable. I understand such things run in families."

Stern shifted impatiently. "Deena seems in control of her faculties."

Helen hesitated. "It did not happen all at once for Lizzy, either. It was a series of little things. I mean, even King George III had many bouts of madness before it advanced so far the Parliament made his son regent. As for Deena, never mind, it's probably nothing."

"What is it, Helen?" Stern was frowning now.

"Deena said she'd rather I didn't spend so much time here." She blinked back tears. "I'm afraid she's jealous of me. Kyle, I've tried to be her friend. I know it's silly, but I fear

Deena has used this cat incident to turn Amy against me."

She looked up at him appealingly from damp lashes. "Kyle, if I am a bother to you, I–I'll just stay home."

"Helen, Deena wouldn't turn Amy against you. I'm certain you misunderstood."

"Of course, Kyle." Giving him a weak smile, Helen got gracefully to her feet. "Thank you, Kyle. You always make everything so much better."

Deena did not see Kyle again until late that afternoon. The painting session had not gone well and Debussy stamped angrily about the room, pulling at the strands of hair he still had on top of his head.

"Terrible! Terrible!" he cried. Amy stifled a giggle. Deena shook her head at the girl, fearing that if Amy laughed out loud, she would follow suit.

Finally, the frazzled painter waved them from the room. They left him sputtering murderous threats on himself, on his painting, and on the world in general. Thankfully, he spoke in French, which Amy did not comprehend.

Deena took the time to catch up with Amy's lessons, which had been curtailed because of the long hours required for the painting. It had been a rather mellow, usual day—until she saw Kyle's troubled visage over the dinner table.

With trepidation, she awaited her husband in her large bed.

Carefully, Kyle sat down on the edge of the bed, his gaze searching. Was she unstable, as Lizzy had been those last weeks? He saw no sign of it. And yet. . .

Lord, what do I say to her? Things seemed to be going so well. Taking Deena's hand, Kyle found it cold. "Deena, did you tell Helen that if she couldn't get along with that cat, she was no longer welcome here?"

"No, it wasn't like that. It's just. . ." Kyle watched Deena as she searched for words. "Helen does upset Amy over her reaction to Gray Lady, though I understand she can't help her fear. But, well. . ." The way she bit her lip made him want to kiss her. "Now that we're married. . .well. . ."

Tracing her jaw with his finger, Kyle stared into her anxious eyes. "Are you saying you prefer more time alone with your new husband?" He rather liked the idea. "I fear you hurt her feelings, my dear."

Deena said softly, "That was not my intent, but—"

Kyle's eyes narrowed. "Helen's been a good friend, to both of us. When she returns tomorrow, I would like it if both you and Amy tendered your apologies."

Deena sat up quickly. "Amy's done nothing wrong."

"I'll not have my daughter turned against her."

"I had nothing to do with it. From what she's told me, Amy never has felt all that comfortable around Helen."

Deena had a point. "Be that as it may, I'd still like you and Amy to apologize."

"That will only make Amy resent her more, Kyle."

Grabbing her, Kyle growled, "I won't have my daughter defying me."

Deena silently rocked away from him.

"Deena, Deena." His hand shook as he touched her cheek, only to have her shrink away from his touch.

Lord, what have I done? I've tried so hard to gain her trust and in one angry moment, I destroyed it all. Jesus, help me!

"Please, Deena. I'm sorry." He knew the true direction of his anger was Lizzy, not Deena. *Forgive me, Lord,* he cried silently as he gathered Deena's trembling body into his arms.

She was so light and he so big and strong. Lying down on the bed, Kyle rocked her in his arms. "I'm sorry, my darling Deena. I am sorry." He said the words over and over as he held Deena's unresponsive form.

It was a long time before her shivering stopped and she lay against him quietly, eyes still closed. They lay in the darkened bedroom in silence; only the crackle of the fire sounded in the room. His eyes sad, he smoothed back her thick hair from her tear-dampened cheeks. "Please look at me, Deena."

He groaned as she opened her eyes. He'd seen eyes like that before. . .on a fawn trapped by a wolf. Weary, frightened, untrusting eyes. "Can you forgive me?"

He let her search his face. Reaching up, she touched the

single tear coursing down his tanned cheek.

"I do. I must." She sighed, looked away. "Because of Lizzy you'll never trust me. . .not truly. Why did you marry me instead of Helen, like she expected?"

"Because I care for you." He hesitated at the bleakness in her eyes.

He sighed. "Mayhap this whole dustup is a vast misunderstanding." He forced a smile. "I suspect Amy is so wrapped up in Gray Lady she resents Helen. And you, wanting to be a good mother to Amy are. . .a bit zealous perhaps."

Kyle patted her shoulder as though she were a naughty child. She stiffened at his touch. Puzzled, he said, "You explain to Helen on the morrow."

Burying her head in her pillow, Deena cried herself to sleep. Just when they had made a tentative move toward each other, something happened. As much as she hated to admit it, she felt part of the problem was Helen.

She well understood his reluctance to tell the lonely widow her constant presence was less than welcome. Unless it wasn't. The thought disturbed Deena.

The next afternoon, Kyle said, "Helen, I am convinced this whole affair is simply a misunderstanding."

Taking in Deena's pale face and puffy eyes, Helen smiled. "Of a certain, Kyle. I do forgive you, dear. I know you didn't mean anything by what you said."

Deena opened her mouth. Nothing came out. Why did the woman have to be so kind?

"What have you to say, Deena?"

"I didn't mean to hurt your feelings, but I still feel—"

Kyle didn't let her finished. "Truth is, Helen, Deena and I do need time alone. I know you understand. As for Amy, I've already told her she may play with Gray Lady only in the kitchens or the nursery."

Deena stilled a sigh. Helen broke the tense silence with a forced laugh. "Now that that's over," she smiled at Kyle, "I have an invitation to extend. A week from Saturday I'm planning to host a reception for the two of you. Just a few close friends and neighbors, you understand."

"Why, that's most gracious of you, Helen. Isn't it, Deena?"

Relieved Helen understood, Deena smiled. "Of course we'll come."

Helen turned toward Deena. "Kyle, have you told your little bride your plans?"

Deena glanced toward Kyle, who had the grace to look uncomfortable. "I fear I've had little opportunity."

Unable to mask her hurt, she asked, "What plans?"

"I too want to hold a reception, say, sometime next month, to formally dedicate the new portrait."

"Isn't that the sweetest thing?" cooed Helen. Deena wanted to cry, for it confirmed for her Kyle's interest in her had been nothing more than kindness and protection.

But they were married. And she was determined to make him a good wife.

Deena straightened her shoulders. "Why, Kyle. I'm sure Amy and I will have fun organizing the reception."

Disconcerted, Helen began, "I can—"

Quickly, Deena smoothed, "I could not possibly impose upon you further, Helen. You'll have quite enough to do with your own reception—right, Kyle?"

He grinned. "Of course, Deena. I'm sure you and Amy will do right well."

Deena wished he'd always look at her with such tenderness.

৯

The breeze swirled warm air about Deena as she leaned against the porch railing of the modest two-story Federal-style house Helen called home. "However little she is here," Deena muttered to herself as she gazed over the well-tended lawns.

Helen had done the inside of the house in a profusion of extravagance. Strangled by the ostentatious decor as well as the seemingly brittle congratulations of the guests, Deena sought the peace and quiet of the balcony. Below, the lawns sloped away into the darkness. The large silver moon peeped out every now and again from the growing banks of dark clouds.

Strains of Bach drifted to Deena through the partially open French doors. Inside the guests chatted softly. Occasionally Deena heard a burst of laughter.

She was not unaware of the looks Kyle received with Helen on one side and her on the other.

Truth to tell, the last week had been relatively mild, though there remained a certain restraint between her and Kyle. Why was he so withdrawn? Was he angry with her for asking Helen to limit her time at Three Oaks?

Though she valued their prayer time together, Kyle seemed to hold himself under extreme control. He scarcely touched her, and when he did, he jerked away as though scalded.

Gray Lady, corralled mainly in the nursery where Helen never intruded, remained undisturbed with her little mistress. Deena fretted about it because Amy seldom ventured out of her rooms. Deena sighed. She would have to speak to Kyle about it.

Clasping the railing, Deena shifted her weight to her good leg. Her long rose gown rustled about her legs as she moved. She was woman enough to relish the admiration in the eyes of her husband when she had presented herself to him earlier. "You are so lovely, Deena."

Brushing a caress against her cheek, he took her arm, attending her carefully into the calash carriage, which he himself drove. He presented a handsome picture in his black formal cutaway jacket, breeches, and buckled shoes.

They rode along in silence. Glancing up at him, Deena was rewarded with a half smile. She responded in kind. Mayhap there was hope. Maybe later, she'd discover what bothered him.

Deep in thought, Deena missed the quiet steps behind her until she felt heat on her neck. Instinctively, Deena turned. At the sight of Helen in her low-cut evening gown of forest green, the anticipation died from Deena's eyes.

"Some say evening air is dangerous," Helen purred.

"Fresh air is invigorating, healthy."

A thin smile spread on Helen's lips. "Ah, we shall soon

see." Her mood changed abruptly. "I wished a moment with you."

Deena tried unsuccessfully to search the older woman's shadowed face. "Why now? You have ample opportunity at Three Oaks. . .every day." She winced at her tone. After all, she wanted Helen to remain a friend.

Strains of one melody ended, and another began in a loud burst that partially drowned Helen's words. "I've tried to be your friend, but it's difficult when you ban me from the house."

"It's just that Kyle and I need time together."

Helen gripped Deena's arm with an intensity that made her gasp. "I need him, too. Don't you understand? I need Kyle."

At Deena's quick intake of breath, Helen laughed softly as she moved forward, forcing Deena back against the railing. "Foolish man married you to protect his reputation, what is left after Lizzy."

Frightened, Deena desperately grabbed the railing. Leaves of the vine entwining the railing disintegrated in Deena's grasp. As if in slow motion, Deena felt herself topple. A moment later she found herself thumped back to the solid flooring.

"Ah, there you are ladies. Having a quiet coz, I see." Helen moved away from Deena, who stumbled against Kyle. Chuckling, Kyle righted her.

Helen reached for his arm. "Your little bride seems to prefer her company to ours."

Kyle's frown reappeared. "That true? Deena, Helen did this for us."

Casting a frightened glance toward Helen's smiling face, Deena shook away the disturbing impression. Surely Helen hadn't deliberately tried to throw her over the railing. Had she? The bruise on her arm was real enough. Deena rubbed it absently. "Kyle, may we go home?"

"Now, Deena, after all Helen's trouble?"

Deena closed her eyes against the threatening tears. "Please, I—I don't feel well."

Concerned, Kyle put an arm about her trembling shoulders. "Yes, of course. Must not permit you to get ill."

"I tried to tell her the night air was dangerous, but you know how these young ones are," Helen soothed.

Concern edged his voice. "Deena, you're far too pale. We'll get you home straightway. Helen, you will tender our regrets."

"Of course, Kyle."

It was with deep-seated relief Deena sat beside Kyle as he tooled the horses out of Helen's driveway. Breathing deeply of the clean crisp air, Deena felt some of the tension leave her.

"Been feeling poorly long?"

"Not long." Overhead, the moon ducked under a cloud.

"I hope this wasn't a trick to get me to take you home. That was the sort of thing Lizzy would do." He paused. "We'll have to visit again soon to make up for tonight."

"No! I mean, I'd rather not. . .go there again."

"Is something wrong?"

Deena rubbed her forehead. She had a very real headache now. She glanced at him sideways. "Helen told me that I have no claim to you save pity." Deena stared over the heads of the horses cantering along smoothly.

She wished she could more rightly judge Kyle's reactions. He was still. Was he listening. . .or angry?

"Go on."

Deena sighed again. "This seems silly now, but I almost thought—for a moment—she was trying to push me over the railing."

Silence. Deadly silence. With effort, Kyle stilled his groan. Was Deena exhibiting the same signs of instability that Lizzy showed toward the last? "You're overwrought," he soothed.

"You're probably right." What else could she say?

Kyle's hands tightened on the reins. As soon as the horses broke stride, Kyle released the reins again as he struggled against the urge to take Deena in his arms. She sounded so lost.

Whatever prompted her fantasy, Deena was a vulnerable young woman—and his wife.

The muscle in his cheek twitched. *Lord, have I made another mistake? I thought this was in Your plan. Now, I don't know.* Glancing over at Deena, he saw her chin tremble. So she was not as calm as she pretended. As the horses cantered around a corner, Deena leaned away from him. Was she frightened of him?

What if she was unstable? What of her influence on Amy? *Lord, show me what to do.*

Love her, came the answer. *Love her.*

"Deena," he spoke slowly, measuring each word. "You're not sure what happened, are you?"

Deena shook her head. "She thought you'd marry her, not me."

Taking a deep breath, he tried to explain. "When Lizzy died, Helen blamed herself. Fact is, Helen insisted on nursing Lizzy through her childbirth and illness. The babe was still-born. Lizzy lost all will to live—she was disoriented, at times even delusional, before she weakened and died. Nothing could be done. Even the doctor said so. Helen cried."

Tears gathered in Deena's eyes. "And you comforted her."

"Yes," said Kyle. "Then her husband died." He hesitated. "This is not general knowledge, and I ask you to keep this to yourself, but—her husband killed himself."

"What did she do?"

"There wasn't much to do. She confessed she tore up the note he left. She made it look accidental. I just let it ride. There had been enough pain and hurt. . .for both of us."

"You really care about her, don't you?"

"Yes, I do." He reached for Deena's hand. "But you're my wife and I want to please you."

She gulped in air quickly. "Even if it means explaining, again, to Helen, I feel I need more time with just us?"

Coming out from behind a bank of clouds, the moon shone down on Deena's hesitant face.

As he pulled up in the driveway at Three Oaks, he sighed, "Don't worry, Deena. I'll explain to Helen."

thirteen

True to his word, Kyle gave Helen the ultimatum—at least Deena assumed as much since she no longer spent much time at Three Oaks.

Amy clapped her hands. "Oh, Mama. Now I don't have to keep Gray Lady in the nursery, do I?"

Seldom able to withstand his daughter's pleas, Stern gave in readily enough. From then on, one scarcely saw the little girl without the cat perched precariously on her shoulder.

If the staff rejoiced, Deena mourned silently, but not for Helen. "Helen asked me about a problem with the drainage of her kitchen," or "Helen wants my advice about one of her horses." Every time she turned around, Helen had another problem Kyle needed to check out. Then there were his business trips to Portsmouth, which kept him away several days at a stretch. It seemed to her he invented reasons to stay away from her.

Deena missed Kyle. Missed his slow smile, missed the tender light in his eyes when he looked at her, missed. . .

Pain twisted inside her. Was he tired of her already? The servants had begun to whisper about the time he spent away from home, time he spent with Helen. At times Deena wondered at her ability to smile, or laugh with Amy—ability to carry on as though everything was normal. Normal? Her life had been anything but normal for a long time.

Even Amy suffered from Kyle's constant absence.

Bitter and sick at heart, Deena continued running the household, continued her lessons with Amy. She even managed to sit for the painting without revealing the depth of her pain, or believed so.

Often she cried herself to sleep. At mealtimes, Deena but picked at the delicious food. Kyle didn't seem to notice.

Since Kyle had not said otherwise, Deena went forward

with plans for the reception feeling the complete hypocrite. How could Kyle hang a portrait of a woman he avoided like Helen avoided cats?

Debussy, however, was beside himself. Marching around the room, he swore loudly about marital spats, decried the dullness of Deena's eyes, the deathly pallor of her skin.

Deena blinked back tears. She should not have weakened and married him. He did not love her. More fool she to think she stood any chance at all against either his hatred for Lizzy, or his longtime affection for Helen.

Lord, what do I do? I love him, but he doesn't seem to care. What more can I do? But she didn't listen for the answer.

Instead, Deena poured her love into Amy, for she loved the girl as her own. For her sake, Deena tried to pretend all was well, but Amy was more observant than Deena gave her credit for. Deena could put up with Kyle's inattention to her, but not to Amy. A hard knot of anger began to grow.

"Papa," Amy confronted her father as they walked together in her favorite garden. "Mama isn't well. And she's sad."

Kyle stopped. "Not well?"

"Mama hardly eats. And Papa, I've heard her crying. What's wrong, Papa? She's not going to die?"

Kyle stared down at Amy. "No, it's nothing like that."

"Then what, Papa? Is it because you are never here anymore? I think Mama misses you."

Sitting down, Kyle gathered his daughter into his arms. Guilt stirred within. How could he explain how it pained him to be near Deena, but not to touch her or hold her? He'd promised himself he'd go slow, and now he had other reasons not to risk intimacy, reasons he could not explain to his daughter. "Mrs. Billings needs me right now, squirrel."

Amy stiffened and pulled away, reminding Kyle sharply of Deena. "She's taking you away!"

Kyle's face whitened. "Stop it! If this is the way your mother is letting you behave, I'll—"

"You won't send her away," she cried. "No, I'll not lose Mama."

Kyle held her close. Amy collapsed in his arms, weeping. "Papa. I'll be good. Please. I'll never do anything bad again. . . just don't make her go away. . .like my other mama. Please!"

Cursing himself silently, Kyle held his hysterical daughter. "Squirrel, I won't. I promise I won't send her away."

As Amy finally calmed, he set her on his knee. "I'll not send your mother away, Amy, but you must promise me not to say bad things about Helen. Does your mother allow you to speak so?"

Amy lifted her tearstained face to his. "Mama never says anything bad about anyone. Papa, I miss you."

Obviously there was more to the situation than he understood. Was Deena ill? Upset? Kyle could not recall having even looked directly at her for days—or was it longer? Had she need of a doctor? A minister?

He quelled the panic simmering inside. Had he been free, he would have immediately sought Deena out. As it was, he spent most of the afternoon reassuring his daughter not only of his love, but of his promise not to send away her mother.

Retreating to his study, Kyle picked up the long baize envelope and slit it open.

The letter began "Dear Kyle and Deena."

Kyle winced at the oneness that opening implied. He had certainly done little enough to improve the situation. How could he explain to Deena how much being around her pained him? How could he tell her how much he feared he would see signs of mental deterioration? And being near her, he feared he would succumb to his need of her.

No, no, a thousand times no. He would not bring another child into the world who might be tainted with madness. He shuddered as he thought of Amy. He would have to watch her as well.

Deena was his wife, and, despite everything, he cared for her. Could never put his delicate wife into any of the horrible places which housed the insane. He would see to her at Three Oaks, at whatever cost. Besides, he promised Amy.

Scanning the letter, he skipped hastily over Andrea's rapture over her upcoming marriage, as well as over the minute details of the arrangements. Toward the end of the letter, he read with a decided frown.

My dear friend, Deena,
How can I ever thank you for smoothing the way for us. Both Daniel and I want you and Kyle to stand up for us as we did for you. Please answer in the affirmative. 'Twould not be the same without you.

Finishing the missive, Kyle sighed. He sighed a lot these days, he decided, as he folded the letter before tucking it into his vest pocket. Sighing more deeply, Kyle went to change for dinner.

Dinner conversation was, at best, stilted. Tonight, however, Kyle scrutinized the woman who had so recently become his wife. Deena flinched from his scrutiny in a way which made Kyle feel like some ogre.

For the first time, Kyle noted the deep lines under her large eyes, her prominent cheekbones. When she stood, her gown hung loosely about her slender body. What in thunderation had he done to her?

As he took her arm to lead her into the familiar family room, Stern felt Deena tremble under his arm. Was she really so terrified of him?

As they settled onto the sofa, Helen sauntered into the room and Kyle rose to greet her. Had Deena but witnessed the irritation in the face of her husband at the interruption, she might have not felt so desolate as Helen possessively took his arm.

"You didn't come over, Kyle," she chided. "Is something amiss?"

She smiled sweetly at Deena. "Your dear husband has been *soo* kind."

That was it! Helen had no intention of letting Kyle go, and from the way her husband acted, Deena couldn't help wonder just how successful the sensuous widow had been. Anger burned, curling around her heart.

Deena rubbed her forehead. "Please excuse me, Helen, Kyle. I fear I have a megrim coming on." She'd been having them as of late. Upstairs, Deena cried herself to sleep.

Kyle, still feeling guilt, as well as concern for his wife, later came to her room. He found her asleep, dried tears on her cheeks. Tenderness for her welled up inside him and he gently stroked her cheek. Jealousy ill became her.

The next morning, Deena was surprised to find Kyle lingering over breakfast. "I thought you'd be gone." Deena's shoulders slumped and what little appetite she had fled. "Might as well get the scold over and done, Kyle?"

"Deena, you have to eat something. You're thin as a rail."

She shrugged. "You wish to scold here, or in your study?" She swayed slightly as she rose to her feet.

Frowning, Stern took her arm. "It was unseemly of you to rush away last night. Your ruse was most obvious."

A cynical smile twisted Deena's lips. "You wish I learn more devious methods?"

"No! That is certainly not what I mean. It isn't as though Helen is here much as of late. You might at least have been polite."

"She had no desire to cling to my arm and stare vacuously into my face." Gone the frightened young woman who winced away from conflict. The woman who faced Kyle was a woman with a stone face and flashing eyes, eyes filled with anger and pain. "Am I to cozen a woman who commands my husband's attendance at the crook of her little finger? When she left, so did you. Why not declare your dalliance to the world? You have the face to denigrate Lizzy, not to mention me, when you bed the neighbor with no by-your-leave to anyone, including your neglected wife. Wife. What a jest!"

"How dare you!" He slammed his fist on the arm of his chair.

"How dare I what?" Deena leaned forward, eyes flashing. "How dare I say to your face what the servants say behind your back? Or don't you care that your daughter waits in vain for scraps of her father's attention?"

"If you have insinuated lies to Amy, I'll—"

"How addlepated do you think I am? Even if you are the biggest scoundrel in the entire world, I would do almost anything to keep that little girl believing in her father. . .the father she loves with all her little heart."

"You're beside yourself, Deena." Kyle's anger had faded, and Deena sensed the accusation hit home.

"Now you think I've an attic to let? What an easy way to rid yourself of my presence. Should have stayed in England, could have gone straight to Bedlam."

"Stop it!" Kyle growled, his anger simmering again. "Helen is not my mistress and never has been. As for you, you are, more often than not, a hysterical female given to fantasy. I mean, thinking Helen meant to throw you over the balcony— really."

"I imagine the two of you have laughed heartily over that one." Deena looked at her husband through cold, dispassionate eyes so different from the large eyes of the innocent girl who first came under Stern's protection.

"It doesn't matter, does it? You'll never trust me, will you, you can't, not when you still haven't forgiven Lizzy for hurting you." Deena slumped against the cushions as exhaustion overtook her. "There never was a chance for us, was there? I wanted to be a wife, but you never wanted me, did you, not really?"

Furious at her accusations, Kyle threw back, "Mayhap, I should have not been quite so hasty. Helen, at least, is not an unstable child."

At his words, Deena jerked to her feet. "Yes, I guess mayhap you should have married her instead." She limped from the room, cursing the leg that refused her bidding at this critical time. Inside she felt shredded.

Almost immediately Kyle regretted his hasty words, but it was too late to call them back, much too late. The devastated look in Deena's eyes as she left him haunted him. Dropping his head into his hands he groaned aloud, *Lord, what have I done?*

How could it have all gone so wrong? He cared for the girl. Cared for her greatly.

So what had gone amiss, and when? Truth to tell, he could not put his finger on it. Had she desired to be his wife in truth? He made her feel unwanted. He groaned again, then started as a clock bonged in the distance.

Reluctantly he rose to his feet. He had promised to meet Helen. Bother! Why had he not realized how run-down her place had become over the last few years? For all the problems, 'twas a good thing sending Helen back to tend her own affairs.

How could he refuse to assist her after her generosity? But Deena was his wife. Amy, he'd neglected as well. And he thought Deena unstable! No, the problem was his own stubbornness. Again he groaned.

He had broken faith with the young woman he had made his wife. That had to change. With that determination, Kyle got into his curricle to explain to Helen.

≈

Princess shied at each puff of wind and quivering leaf. *Probably,* thought Deena, *the mare senses my agitation.*

She rode alone in order to sort out her thoughts; alone to pray; alone to cry. Galloping along, Deena lifted her face to the stiff breeze against her tear-streaked cheeks.

Entering a wood, Deena let the mare pick her way down an almost nonexistent path. Overhead in the branches, birds trilled, and the underbrush rustled with a host of small unseen varmints. Strange sounds emanated from the forest, making Deena start. A bear? Snakes? Indians? Phooey! As if any of those things mattered now.

Her thoughts tumbled over and over. Helen. Always Helen. Why not leave and let Kyle have his dear Helen? She sat up. Kyle had said her accusations were but lies. Whatever made her think Helen tried to seduce him? Mayhap EverPine did need work. For once she recognized her feelings for Helen for what they were, jealousy.

The problem was not Helen, but her own overactive imagination. How much had the woman who befriended her suffered under Deena's unjust condemnation? *Lord, forgive me.*

She felt her weakness from lack of proper nourishment and

sleep. Did that not give credence to the idea she was unbalanced? Poor Kyle. She knew her fears communicated to Amy, leaving the little girl anxious. That would not do.

She thought then of Kyle, her husband. They began married life with hope of a future. She thought, at times, he cared for her. Examining her thoughts, her feelings, Deena knew, despite everything, she loved him.

Determination flashed in Deena's eyes. If there was hope, any hope at all, she would fight. No more moping. No more tears. She would be Kyle's wife. Hopefully, Orrin's letter would soon come. That too would help set things right between them.

Praying and planning, Deena paid scant attention to Princess's direction. Ahead, a wide, shallow stream gurgled and splashed along a rocky bed. The path widened, trees gave way to a meadow.

Suddenly, from the security of the last tall tree, a tawny beast growled. Whinnying in panic, the little mare broke into a dead run. It all happened so unexpectedly, Deena was unseated. Trying to regain her balance, she lost hold of a rein.

The loose rein, flapping alongside the mare's neck, sent the skittish animal into a new frenzy. She raced toward the stream. Deena felt the mare's muscles bunch, ready to leap.

At the last moment, the mare skidded to an abrupt halt. Deena, losing her tenuous hold, sailed over the mare's nose headfirst into the stream. Her head hit a large flat boulder and wedged just above the water.

Stepping gingerly into the icy stream, Princess nuzzled her mistress, then shied at the red liquid trickling down her face. Deena shivered in the cold water and lay still.

Puzzled, Princess paced back and forth, periodically nudging her mistress. There was no response. Finally, as the afternoon shadows lengthened, Princess swung about and galloped back toward the safety of her stable.

fourteen

"Papa! Papa!" Amy cried, running into the entry hall.

Amy's welcoming smile gladdened his weary heart, especially since Helen had been less than understanding about spending less time at EverPine.

Winding her little arms about her father's neck, Amy gazed anxiously down into his face. "Oh, Papa, I haven't seen Mama all day. Isn't she with you?"

Kyle's arms tightened about Amy. "No, squirrel, she went riding after I saw her this morning."

"She loved riding with you, Papa."

He sighed as the weight of his guilt increased.

Momentarily, Kyle's anger flared. How dare Deena absent herself from Amy? Did she think to punish him thus? "Mayhap Esie can tell us where she is."

Amy shook her head. "No one has seen her. I asked." Tears glistened in her eyes. "You must find her, Papa. You must find my mama! She would not leave me. She loves me."

Suddenly, Esie's husband burst in. "Master Stern."

Irritation showed in Kyle's eyes. "What is it, Crooks?"

"Princess returned," he paused for breath, "she returned without the mistress."

Visions of Deena's pale, anguished face floated before him. "Are you telling me my wife never returned from her ride?"

At the truth in the groom's eyes, Kyle groaned. "Who went with her?" he demanded.

Crooks shifted uncomfortably. "She wished to ride alone."

"Alone," Kyle echoed, hugging Amy, who began to cry. "Why ever did you permit such a thing?"

He knew his harsh accusation was more directed at himself than the white-faced groom. "My apologies, Dale."

"I understand," said the groom, eyeing his master.

Amy tugged on her father's neck to get his attention. "Papa. You must find Mama. What if she is hurt? What if—"

"No, Amy. She is not. . .she can't." *Oh Lord, no!* he cried silently. "Crooks, saddle the horses."

"Right, sir." He turned to go, but Esie, just entering the room, grabbed his arm.

"What is it? Mrs. Stern's missing, isn't she?" Fear mixed with condemnation in her eyes as she looked from her husband to Stern.

Crooks squeezed her hand. "We're going out now."

Kyle handed Amy into her care. "See to Amy. Don't leave her alone!"

She waited while Kyle tried to comfort his daughter. "Amy, I'll do everything I can to bring your mother home safely. God willing, I'll bring her back."

As he swung aboard his roan, his heart thudded sickeningly. Suddenly his suspicions, his anger, faded in the light of dawning truth. He loved Deena, loved her in a way he had never loved any other woman. . .or ever could. Dear Lord, what had he done to her. . .to them? Deena was right, he had never given them a chance. He hadn't given her a chance because Lizzy always stood between them.

Along with the stable hands, Kyle spread out to search the estate. In the growing darkness his guilt crushed down on him as he visualized every angry word he had spoken. Only this time he saw more than a stubborn child, he saw Deena as the vulnerable, frightened young woman under his care who had tentatively reached out for his love only to have him reject her again and again.

He examined his relationship with Helen through her eyes. Deena had reason to be jealous when he spent so much time with the winsome neighbor. True, EverPine needed work, but his absence had more to do with keeping himself from temptation. He ached to hold Deena, yet fear kept him at bay.

Helen was wrong. The thought startled him and he groaned aloud. "Jesus, keep her safe. Forgive me!"

He prayed as he rode, begging for time to make things right.

He stared up into the sky, now twinkling with stars. Scavengers rustled in the underbrush. A fox scurried across his path.

Ahead, he heard the gurgle of the stream marking the end of his property. Breaking into a trot, the roan stopped at the edge to drink. Absently, Kyle patted his neck.

Overhead, the night sky rumbled a warning as a cold breeze whipped his cape. "Oh Lord, help us find her soon."

The roan shied. "Steady, boy." As Kyle stared into the stream, something moved. In a flash, Kyle swung from the roan and waded into the icy water.

He stared into the still face of his wife. "Deena!" Tenderly, he gathered her chilled body into his arms. "My darling."

Splashing to the bank, Kyle lay his wife on the ground. Taking off his cape, he bent to wrap it about her shivering body. Hesitated. Putting down the cape, Kyle gingerly stripped off her sodden clothes. Even in his urgency he took note of her maturing body. Gulping, Kyle wrapped her firmly in his cape.

Before picking her up, he reached for his rifle, firing shots into the air to let the others know he was bringing her in.

Cradling her in his arms aboard the roan, he headed for home. In the darkness, the roan eagerly made his way back to the warmth of his stable, leaving Kyle focused on the lovely young woman in his arms.

He had never envisioned how lovely she was. Hers was not the body of a child—had she not told him thus? Helen was wrong. . .again.

Closing his eyes, Kyle vowed. "Deena, we'll start anew. If you will but give me the chance."

Feeling a trickle on his arm, he looked down and was appalled at the flow of blood from her forehead. In the stream the icy water had kept the flow at a minimum, washed it away.

To his alarm, the blood flowed faster, soaking into his jacket. To stem the flow, Kyle held her tightly to his chest.

Near Three Oaks, Crooks galloped up. "Praise the Lord! You found her!"

"Ride for the doctor, Crooks. Make it fast."

Crooks swung the bay about and galloped off even before Kyle finished speaking.

Sliding off the roan, Kyle strode into the house.

Esie followed him up the stairs to Deena's bedchamber. She turned down the covers and threw a protective cover over the clean sheets before Kyle lay Deena down.

He jerked the other covers over Deena's shaking form. "More covers, Esie." Turning, he saw Enid hovering just outside the doorway. "Lay a fire," he ordered.

Esie pushed Kyle toward the door to his room. "Go. Get out of those wet clothes or you'll catch yourself the death of cold. We need not have two to tend. Your wife needs us."

When the doctor arrived, Stern, dressed in tan pantaloons and maroon jacket sans cravat (evidence of his hasty toilet), met him in Deena's bedchamber.

"My wife is here, Dr. Meyer." He showed the white-haired man to the bed. 'Twas not but three years hence he had done the same for Lizzy. He gulped. Would the outcome be the same? *God, no!*

Kyle paced the room during the doctor's examination. After tending to Deena's head wound, the doctor turned. Kyle stopped his pacing. "Well, Doctor?"

"Your wife is very ill. The fall and the time spent in the water did her little good. She looks to be in the first stages of pneumonia.

"Also," the doctor tugged his earlobe, "she has a concussion. It be not good she has not awakened. Don't know what to tell you. We know so little of head injuries." He paused. "She'll need constant care. Not to be left alone."

"Depend on it, Dr. Meyer," Stern said firmly.

Esie stepped forward. "Please, sir, if you'll permit me."

Enid stepped up beside her, "And me."

Stern nodded. "Of course. Doctor, what are we to do?"

Dr. Meyer gave instructions with an exactness and with enough warning to give Kyle pause. In a smooth hand, Kyle wrote out the doctor's directions and laid them by the bed.

"If there is any change, good or bad, send for me." The

doctor handed Esie a vial. "Give her this should she seem in pain, but not more than four times a day. Keep her warm. If she awakens, get her to take liquids." He tugged his earlobe again, his blue eyes solemn as he looked over at Deena. "I'll be back on the morrow." With a nod to Stern, he took his leave.

Stern stared down at his wife, grief etching his face. Esie touched his arm. "I'll see to her."

"Papa!" Amy ran to her father's waiting arms as he entered the nursery. "Did you find Mama? Is she all right?"

Kyle hugged his daughter. She had always believed in Deena. At his look, Mrs. Cairns quietly left the room.

Kyle sat down on a large rocker with Amy on his knees. "We found your mother, Amy. She's alive."

Amy bounced up and down. "Let's go see her!"

"Not now, squirrel." He hesitated. "Your mama is very ill."

"She will be all right, won't she, Papa?"

Kyle's voice broke. "Oh, Amy. I don't know."

"We must pray for her. God loves Mama. I love Mama. We must pray real hard. God will hear us?" It was a question.

"Yes, God hears. I just don't know how He'll answer."

With that, Amy burst into tears. As Stern held her close, his own tears mingled with those of his daughter.

After dinner, Kyle entered Deena's bedchamber. "Off to bed with you, Esie," he said. "I'll tend my wife now."

As she left, Stern gathered Deena's feverish body into his arms and held her close. At first she struggled against him, then, murmuring incoherently, snuggled close.

Kyle continued to hold her until he dozed off. Startled awake, he lay Deena against the covers.

"Kyle!" she cried out.

After a moment's consideration, Kyle slid out of his gold braid trimmed burgundy robe and slipped under the covers beside his wife. As he enfolded her in his arms, she sighed. He smiled as he too drifted off to sleep.

Esie took over in the morning. Restless and feverish, Deena soaked the covers. Esie sponged her hot, yet shivering body while Kyle stood by hesitantly.

"Leave her to me, I'll take care of her like she is my own."

With reluctance, Kyle went to dress. If only she would awaken.

Still musing on the night, he descended the stairs only to hear a familiar, and at the moment, not a particularly welcome voice.

"Where's Mr. Stern?" Helen demanded.

Kyle stopped. He had little desire to see Helen this morning. *Must she always be so possessive?* The thought startled him as he realized the truth of the matter. It gave credence to Deena's jealousy. Helen *was* possessive. He frowned. Why had he not seen it before?

Helen saw him then or he would have gone back to his room, back to Deena. "Helen."

She grasped his arm. "Oh, Kyle. How is the dear child?"

"Child? Speak you of my wife?"

"No need to get upset, though goodness knows you have right to be upset. Going off on her own like that."

Kyle wiped a tired hand across his brow. "That's enough, Helen. My wife is an excellent horsewoman. 'Twas an accident only, 'tis my fault. I should have been riding with her."

"I'm sorry," Helen murmured. "I'm just worried. You must let me help. After all, this is partly my fault. If I hadn't insisted you make all those repairs at EverPine. . ."

He hesitated long enough for Helen to continue. "How is she?"

"Not well." Anguished sorrow crossed his face. "Deena has pneumonia and a concussion."

"Is she conscious?" Helen asked quickly.

Riffling his fingers through his hair, Kyle sighed. "No. Doc says she needs constant care."

Helen sucked in a breath. "Kyle, you must let me help."

Kyle stared down at her with a dispassion at her tight lips. "Best you go home."

Tears sprang into her eyes. "Dear Kyle, I know I've caused dissension between you two. I was so used to having you to lean on since. . .since. . .Ralph—" She gulped. "Please let me make amends. Let me tend to her. . .as I did Lizzy."

"Esie's nursing her now."

Helen grasped his arm. "But she has so many other duties. Let me do this for you."

"There is Enid."

Helen scoffed. "What does she know of nursing? But I, I have experience in these matters."

Kyle's irritation faded into thoughtfulness. "I don't know."

Helen smiled then. "Kyle, don't worry. I'll take care of everything, just like I did for Lizzy."

Though Esie was less than pleased to see Helen, there was little she could do but give way to the woman who took over the sickroom.

Esie muttered angrily as she departed. Down-stairs, she called Enid to her side. "That Billings woman is taking over the sickroom. I want you up there. I mislike that woman."

The next afternoon, Enid shared afternoon tea with Helen. An hour or so later, Enid left for her own quarters, deathly ill.

Dr. Meyer spoke to Kyle. "Looks like indigestion. It isn't a bad case, though. Enid will be up and about soon."

His visit to Deena was less encouraging. He checked her pulse. Examined her head. "She has not awakened?"

"No, Doctor."

The doctor frowned at the presence of the lovely neighbor. "You've been keeping her warm?"

"Of course. I'm tending her the same way I did her sister." Helen shrugged.

His eyes grew thoughtful. "Puzzling case that."

"They are sisters," said Helen tentatively.

"Not the same, not the same at all." Dr. Meyer pulled on his earlobe.

"Don't concern yourself overmuch, Doctor," Helen soothed. "I shall be here to tend her."

Helen had just reached for a thick quilt to cover Deena when Kyle reentered the room. "I just spoke with the doctor." Kyle moved to the bed. Reaching out, he touched Deena's pale cheek.

Though Helen stepped back, she did not leave him alone with Deena. Kyle sensed her presence behind him as he sat down and stroked back Deena's damp hair with a tender hand. With effort, he kept himself from dismissing Helen while he spent time with his wife. After all, she cared, too. "Get well, my darling, I need you. Amy needs you."

Clearing her throat, Helen said, "I shall do all I can."

Kyle nodded absently. "Let's pray for her, Helen."

"You pray, Kyle. I need to see about something." She closed the door behind her, leaving Kyle blessedly alone with Deena.

Bowing his head, he began to pray. "Lord, I bring my concern for Deena to you. Please touch her with Your loving hands and heal her. Heal her quickly, Jesus," his voice wavered, "we need her. . ."

When Kyle again returned to the sickroom later, he found Helen directing the placing of a cot near the hearth. "What's this?"

She stroked his arm. "This is so I can watch over little Deena during the night."

"Helen, I can handle that." Anticipation showed in his eyes.

"Kyle, you need your sleep."

"It's no problem, truly. You have enough to do during the day tending my wife."

Helen grimaced. "Oh, Kyle," she managed a sob. "I want to do this for you. I failed with Lizzy."

Kyle frowned. Helen had been crushed when Lizzy died, how could he gainsay her a chance to redeem herself, not in his eyes, but in her own. Reluctantly he nodded. But, he didn't like leaving Deena, not by half.

For a time he sat at her bedside stroking her hair, her cheek. "Deena, darling. Come back to me. Come back!"

At the connecting door he halted, turned back. "If you need anything at all."

Helen smiled sweetly. "I know, call." She waited for him to leave. Still smiling, she headed for the window. Stopped as Enid entered.

"What do you want?"

"Esie sent me to assist you."

"I need no help. Besides, I thought you were ill."

"I feel fine. Esie says I must stay." Enid firmly ensconced herself in the room.

Sighing, Helen cared for Deena. Bathing her fevered face and neck, changing the linens as they soaked with Deena's sweat, covering her when she shivered with chills.

Enid brought broth and tea which she forced down Deena's throat. Helen kept watch, interfering only as she thought necessary.

Then Enid began dropping the trays, stumbling as she came into the room. Again and again Helen chided the girl for her carelessness, leaving Enid in tears. Whether out of exhaustion or what, Helen left things lying about, always moved just at the right. . .or wrong moment, bumping into the inexperienced maid.

Finally, Helen began fixing tea herself in the room with hot water she had brought up for the purpose. She was all consideration as she spooned it down Deena's throat. Enid continued feeding Deena broth and water.

When Kyle visited, Helen soothed the worried lines on his face.

Some five days later, Deena awoke. Her body leaden, she gazed about the room. Frowning, she tried to remember. . .the argument, Princess. . .falling. She felt hot, so hot.

"Water," she croaked. Deena's eyes widened as Helen held the glass to her lips. She allowed Deena scarcely enough to coat her aching throat.

"More," said Deena.

"Enough for now." Helen set the glass down.

"Dr. Meyer said she was to drink as much as possible," said Enid.

Deena flinched at the dislike Helen flashed the young maid. "Don't get in a taking, Enid. I know what I'm about."

"I'll summon the doctor then."

"He'll be along this afternoon. No need hurrying him along."

"But. . ."

"You're welcome to leave. I could find a much more able assistant."

The girl reddened. "Enid. . .stays." Deena coughed.

Hurriedly Helen allowed her more water. Even as she took the glass away, Deena made herself heard. "Enid stays."

The effort to make her wishes known exhausted her. "Fine, Deena, dear," agreed Helen to calm her.

Deena heard not. She was already asleep.

"Mrs. Stern. Mrs. Stern." The command summoned her.

Deena struggled against the fog surrounding her, dragging her down.

Her eyes opened, focused slowly on a graying man bending over her. "Ah, you're awake. Good." A kind face smiled down at her. Deena relaxed under the gentle hands.

As he undid the bandage at her head, she winced.

"Healing nicely. Good." He looked down into her eyes, frowned. "Time you awoke. Had us worried." He felt her forehead. "Somewhat feverish, and your eyes aren't clear. I don't like that, still. . ."

His smile appeared a trifle forced. "You'll have to take it easy for a long time."

"Aye, Doctor." She smiled then, rather lopsided, but yet a smile.

Helen came up beside the doctor. "Doctor, I'm taking good care of her."

Deena's heart sank. It hadn't taken Helen long to establish herself in the house. She fought feelings of unease. She needed to get up, needed to straighten things out between them. "When may I get up?"

The doctor shook his head. "We'll see about that next time."

Helen waited until the doctor left. "Enid, bring up some fresh water and extra cups. I think Mr. Stern and I should celebrate."

From the maid's expression, Deena knew Enid heartily disliked the rather haughty aristocratic Helen; nonetheless, she left to do Helen's bidding. "I'll tell the others Mrs. Stern's awake and expected to recover."

To Deena, it seemed forever before the maid returned with the teapot and cups on a tray as well as a plateful of newly baked scones.

As Enid departed, Helen plumped the pillows behind Deena. A question lurked in Deena's eyes.

"How long have you been here?"

The muscles of Helen's lips tightened perceptively. "Almost from the first, dear. Kyle needed my help."

"Helen, about the way I treated you. . ." Deena could not keep the note of weariness from her voice.

A wan smile touched Helen's lips. "Don't you worry about that now. You really shouldn't have taken off all alone as you did."

Deena winced at the accusation. "I know. Rather senseless of me, wasn't it." It wasn't a question.

Helen showed even white teeth. "Be that as it may, right now you have a disillusioned husband on your hands."

Deena sighed. "I have made rather a muddle of things, haven't I?"

"You confirmed Kyle's suspicions about you. He wondered about your stability and you go off like that. Deena, Kyle isn't a man who trusts easily. He doesn't need another Lizzy on his hands."

"I'm not like Lizzy, I wouldn't—"

"Maybe not in her morals, though there was Clyde. . ." When Deena shuddered, her erstwhile friend hurried on. "Sorry. But you realize Lizzy was given to fits of temper when she'd be unpredictable and at the end, well. . ."

Deena grimaced at the implication. "Kyle trusts you."

"Because I worked hard to earn that trust and so must you, Deena. You must do everything you can to act normal. Otherwise. . ."

Helen's right, Deena thought. Why shouldn't Kyle trust Helen, the epitome of practical advice and warmth. Pursing her lips, Deena looked away. If only she could be sure of herself. She forced a smile as Kyle followed Enid into the room.

"Dearest Deena." Taking her hand, he gazed into her face with such tenderness her heart pounded.

As usual, Helen interrupted. "Here's the tea!" she exclaimed brightly. Taking the tray, she carried it to a far table and fussed over it.

"You look tired." Timidly, Deena traced the lines in Kyle's face as he sat on the edge of the bed.

"Now, that's what I should be saying to you." He stroked her soft cheek. "I've missed you. I am sorry. I want you to get well so I can make things up to you. . .things will be different. I promise."

Deena believed him. "I too am sorry." She glanced toward Helen. The things she needed to say required privacy, something Helen seemed unwilling to give them. Deena felt too exhausted to ask it of her.

"How's Amy?"

Kyle smiled. "She worries about you, but is otherwise fine. We've both been worried about you."

Carrying the tray, Helen interrupted. "There we are." She set it down on the bed table with no by-your-leave, drew up a chair for herself, and poured out the tea before sitting down.

Practically in Kyle's lap, Deena thought jealously, then scolded herself silently for her uncharitable thoughts. After all, Kyle's eyes were for her alone.

Deftly, Helen took control of the conversation, steering it to herself, leaving Deena frustrated. Why ever would Kyle prefer her over the graceful widow?

Lord, I don't understand. I'm trying not to let this jealousy eat at me, but I feel uncomfortable around Helen.

Deena's tea tasted like dust and she would have put it aside but for Kyle. "I want you strong and well, Deena."

Lying back down, Deena blinked, tried to clear her vision. Fear swelled inside as the room swayed, blurred. She reached out a hand to Kyle. "Kyle, help me," she cried, gripping his arm.

His response sounded like a haunting, disembodied spirit. "Deena, what is it? What's wrong?"

"Everything's blurry, spinning." She could scarcely form the words.

Kyle held Deena to him. "Helen, send for Dr. Meyer. Now!"

Helen leaped to do his bidding. In this new frightening world, Deena clung to Kyle, whose eyes darkened with concern.

It was two hours before the doctor was able to attend them. He hurried into the room with a stride belying his age. Deena, still in Kyle's arms, lay in restless slumber.

"What is it, Mr. Stern?"

Behind them, Helen spoke. "She became delusional. Said the room was spinning."

Dr. Meyer frowned, "I don't like this by half." Gently, he awakened Deena. She stared up at him through dilated eyes. "Dr. Meyer!"

He probed her head. "Tell me what happened."

Deena glanced about the room. Beside Kyle, Helen looked at her with a particular intensity in her eyes that frightened her. Was Helen searching for signs of instability? She stammered, "Things just went spinning, blurry. I'm fine now."

"What had you just to eat or drink before this little episode?"

"Tea." She glanced toward Helen for confirmation.

"I see, mayhap."

Helen interrupted. "Doctor, Mr. Stern and I drank tea from the same pot." The doctor glanced at Kyle for confirmation. Kyle nodded.

"Then I don't know." He tugged on his earlobe. "Head injuries are always difficult."

Deena sat up, then sank back weakly. "Doctor, what happened to me?"

"I wish I knew." He patted her shoulder.

"I will be all right."

"I think so. . .with time."

Reading uncertainty on Kyle's face, Deena sighed. Something was wrong, very definitely wrong. Turning away, Deena hid her tears.

fifteen

"Enid," Helen handed over the tray. "Bring up a fresh pot of water for tea."

Taking the tray, Enid turned straight into Helen's arm. Helen's quick action saved her from a tumble.

"See that, Kyle!" Helen raised her eyes in exasperation. "She continually trips over her own feet. Who knows when she'll stumble and pour hot tea or broth over your little wife?"

Frowning, Kyle watched Deena in restless slumber. Once more she was fast asleep when he visited, as she had been these past several days. She slept so much these days.

Helen took his arm. "If Enid harmed her, I'd never forgive myself. After all, Dr. Meyer says Deena is not to be upset. . . and. . .and, she is so weak." She caught a sob in her throat, causing Kyle to absently put a comforting arm about her shoulders.

"You can't nurse her both day and night, Helen."

Passing a hand over her forehead, Helen leaned against him. "Dear Kyle, you're right, but I cannot leave your precious wife with Enid. Don't get in a taking, Kyle, but I'd like to bring Mrs. Bitley in."

Kyle stiffened. Helen hurriedly explained. "I know she was ill-equipped to handle the household, but she did tend to her husband before he died. I could really use her assistance."

Stern stared down at Deena, mulling the suggestion.

Suddenly, Deena all but sat up in bed, her eyes wide but unseeing. "No, Clyde. *No!*"

Leaping to her side, Kyle gathered her to his chest, murmuring endearments and comfort until Deena calmed in his arms.

In the warmth of her husband's arms, Deena drowsily opened her eyes. Over his shoulder, she beheld a certain anguish on Helen's face. Blocking her out, Deena hid her face against Kyle. With wonder, she savored the comfort of his arms. "Darling, it's all right. 'Twas just a dream."

Looking down at her, he smiled. "You're awake. Good."

Closing her eyes, she drew on his strength. If only she could explain her fears—but there seemed little rationale for the terror which gripped her. What if Helen was right and she was unstable? Helen was wrong. She had to be wrong!

Still and all, that night at EverPine as well as her run-ins with Clyde haunted her nightmares. "There's nothing to fear, darling. You'll be fine," Kyle said, adding, "Debussy has finished the portrait."

Deena looked up. "Amy so wanted to see it."

Kyle smiled. "She has, darling. How about if I bring it up for you to see?"

"I'd like that." Deena's eyes sparkled. Kyle sucked in a deep breath.

Helen interrupted. "Kyle, I think little Deena has had enough excitement."

"But I just got here," Kyle protested as he reluctantly released her.

Deena wanted to rail against Helen, but tantrums only made them think her ready for Bedlam. That frightened her.

"You get well, Deena." Kyle squeezed her hand.

To her consternation, when she tried to smile, a single tear made its way down her cheek.

Disconcerted, Kyle brushed it away with his thumb. "I'll be back to see you later. I promise." He hesitated, plunged on. "Would you like to see Amy?"

"Oh, yes, please! And Gray Lady."

Helen frowned. "I don't think. . ."

Kyle waved her caution aside. "If the doctor agrees, Amy shall see her mother." With that, he strode from the room.

Scarcely did the door close behind him when Helen sniffed, "You know how I feel about that mangy cat."

Deena shivered, but held her gaze. "When she visits, why don't you take a break?" Helen's presence, ever watchful, had begun to unnerve her.

When Enid entered the room, Deena watched icy calm

replace Helen's teary visage. The woman even managed to thank Enid as she took the tray. At a far table, she busied herself steeping the tea.

"Here we go." She held the mug and waited as Deena drank.

"Seems strong," Deena commented, then shivered under Helen's watchful gaze.

"My hand. . .it's so heavy," Deena mumbled. Weakness pervaded her being in a frightening new way. The room blurred, distorted before her heavy eyes. Slumping to one side, Deena slept.

A strident sound startled her awake. Deena focused on the beady eyes staring down at her. "Mrs. Bitley."

"I be yer new nurse, ma'am." Her lips stretched into a travesty of a smile. "Mrs. Billings, she be awake."

Helen came to stand beside the bed; her lips also smiled, though her eyes remained alert. "And how do we feel?"

Deena swallowed. "Dreadful. Water. . .please." It was an effort to speak. The two women exchanged knowing nods.

"Kyle?"

"He's busy." Helen held a mug to Deena's lips. "Drink this now, like a good girl."

Deena chaffed at being treated like a child, but did as she was told. She must needs get strong enough to leave her bed. Instead, nightmares haunted her sleep, terror raced after her. Weak, she was so weak. Her throat screamed for liquid, but when she drank the dryness only increased. Her lips cracked from dryness, her voice croaked the few times she spoke.

"Drink this," she heard again and again.

Deep in her mind she tried to pull herself together. Tried to reach out to speak to Dr. Meyer. Had to tell him something was dreadfully amiss. Her words came out in a gasping mutter.

From far off she heard Helen. "She's delusional."

No! No! Nothing came out of her open mouth.

Kyle, his face grave, held her. She tried to tell him. "It's all right, darling," he croaked.

"Just like Lizzy." Was that Helen?

"Must run in the family," said Mrs. Bitley.

So weak. Must fight. *God, help me! Help me!*

Dr. Meyer paced the study floor. "I don't understand it. I just don't understand. I was certain she was coming out of it."

Kyle hesitated. "Can Helen be correct?"

The doctor tugged his earlobe. "Can't say with any certainty. There are symptoms in common. Weakness, restlessness, the dry throat."

"What about the delusion of danger? Lizzy was much the same toward the end."

"To be sure, but that might be happenstance, and brought on in a completely different way." Dr. Meyer paced. "Have the sisters much in common?"

Kyle shook his head. "Very little, Doctor. They are—were—as different as two persons could be." He wiped a hand across his brow. "What can I do, Doctor?"

"She needs some reason to live. If she continues to get weaker. . ." He gave his earlobe a particularly vicious tug.

"No!" Kyle turned away to hide his expression of sorrow and guilt from the sharp eyes of the doctor. "I must do something," he muttered. He swung back to face the doctor.

"She fair dotes on Amy. Would it be all right if Amy sees her? I. . .I had also planned a reception before all this to introduce a portrait of her and Amy."

"Sounds like reasons to hold on to me, but don't plan that party too far hence," the doctor cautioned.

That afternoon, Kyle was surprised to find Deena awake, if drowsy and weak. Her fawnlike gaze tore at his heart.

He forced a smile. "Surprise, darling." At the wave of his hand, two servants bore a large canvas into the room.

Deena stared at the portrait. "Lovely," she forced out. She closed her eyes as the servants carried it out again.

Though concerned about Deena's lack of response, Kyle gave no sign. "Dear, the reception is set for Saturday next." He squeezed her hand. "I want you up and about. Won't be much of an unveiling without my lovely wife."

Deena gulped, tried to speak. Seeing her effort, Kyle got

her water and helped her drink. The liquid seemed to ease her throat and Deena managed a thin smile. "I. . .I'll try."

"I have another surprise, darling." This time a subdued Amy sidled into the room clutching Gray Lady.

From across the room, Helen cried, "Get that thing out of here!"

"No!" The cry came out as a whisper, but Kyle heard. He had every intention of pandering to his wife.

"Helen, Mrs. Bitley, please leave us."

Under Kyle's uncompromising gaze, Helen shrugged. "As you wish, Kyle. I'll take a break. Mrs. Bitley can take hers later."

It was a small victory, but Deena's eyes brightened. "Amy?"

"Yes, Mama." Awkwardly, Amy stood beside the bed.

"Don't I get a hug?" Deena forced the words.

"Oh, Mama!" Letting the cat down, Amy threw her arms about her mother. Kyle, seeing tears of happiness in Deena's eyes, congratulated himself for permitting the visit.

As Amy released Deena, she pleaded, "Please get well, Mama. Please, get well." Tears welled up in her eyes. "Don't leave me like my other mother."

Her brokenhearted plea did much to restore Deena's will. She swallowed, glanced at the glass beside the bed table. Reaching for it, Kyle gave her another drink. It tasted so good.

"Amy, I will try. I promise." She felt exhaustion enveloping her. She felt Kyle's hand on hers, saw the tenderness in his eyes, and relaxed as she had not been able to relax in ever so long. As Amy rambled on about her activities, Deena desperately tried to stay awake. Though tired, it surprised her how alert she felt this forenoon.

Glancing toward the window where sunshine streamed in, she breathed in fresh air, smelled sweet apple blossoms, heard the birds chirping, squirrels scolding.

"Mama, can I read to you? I've been practicing." Deena did not try to correct her grammar. She just smiled, then frowned as Mrs. Bitley swooped like some bird of prey.

"We don't want Mrs. Stern to get overtired, now do we? I think it best if. . ."

"All the pussyfooting around hasn't done my wife near as much good as this one visit from her daughter. She hasn't looked this well in over a week."

"Mayhap 'tis but a passing thing," Mrs. Bitley suggested.

"Let's hope not. In any case, Amy may visit her mother when she wishes. Is that clear?"

Muttering angrily, the former housekeeper marched to the far side of the room.

"Kyle, that woman frightens me." Deena wondered if she truly dared speak her mind.

"Helen needed help. She thought. . ." Before he could finish, Deena turned her head. Gently, Kyle turned her head back. "Then, she won't stay. I should explain, however, Helen will not have Enid about. The girl is too clumsy."

Deena frowned. Enid had not been that way before. "Esie would help." She hurried on before Kyle could object. "Enid might help downstairs. Please, I trust Esie." As much as she wanted to see a little less of Helen as well, Deena didn't want to burden Kyle further with her care.

He stared into her pleading eyes. "I've failed you before, darling, but not this time."

Deena choked back tears of relief. "Thank you," she whispered. "Thank you."

Reaching for her leather Bible on the stand beside the bed, he flipped it open to Psalm 23. In deep, soothing tones he read, "The Lord is my shepherd; I shall not want. He maketh me to lie down in green pastures, he leadeth me beside the still waters. He restoreth my soul: he leadeth me in the paths of righteousness for his name's sake. Yea, though I walk through the valley of the shadow of death, I will fear no evil: for thou art with me; thy rod and thy staff they comfort me.

"Thou preparest a table before me in the presence of mine enemies: thou anointest my head with oil; my cup runneth over. Surely goodness and mercy shall follow me all the days of my life, and I will dwell in the house of the Lord for ever."

Closing the Bible, he returned it to its place before taking her in his arms. Bowing, he began to pray.

She found herself whispering her own prayer against the smoothness of his jacket as he held her to him. The words "I will fear no evil: for thou art with me" rang in her mind comfortingly.

"Deena," he hesitated before adding, "my darling, get well." Releasing her, he stood. "Amy?"

"Let me stay, Papa."

"All right. But if your mother tires, you must leave."

"Right, Papa." Smiling, Amy hugged her mother before sitting down on the bed.

Kyle motioned for Mrs. Bitley. "Come with me, please."

Reluctantly, she followed him. At the door, she called back. "Mrs. Stern, you must drink the tea we fixed for you before it gets too cold. Miss Amy, run get it. That's a girl." With a strange smile, she left the room.

Amy sniffed at the mug in her hands. "Do you really want this, Mama?"

"No, it is rather nasty, but what else might we do with it?" She dimly recalled refusing the tea during the night and having it spilled mostly down her front as Mrs. Bitley tried to force it down. She left her in her wet gown until just before Kyle's visit.

"I know!" Getting the wash basin, Amy diluted the tea with enough water to cool it before setting it on the floor.

Gray Lady lapped it up, then sat on her haunches to lick herself. As they watched, the cat's movements slowed, became erratic. Meowing pitifully, she dropped into an ungainly huddle.

Amy ran to the cat. "Gray Lady! Mama, what's wrong?"

The cat twisted restlessly in her unnatural sleep. The cat was drugged, drugged with tea meant for her!

Deena shivered. "Guess that tea was stronger than we thought. Think you could find a place to dump the rest of it?" Deena fought exhaustion as questions jumbled in her troubled mind. Two questions demanded answers: Who? and Why?

Glancing from the cat to her mother, Amy's eyes widened. "The flowers. Papa has fresh flowers sent up every morning." Suiting actions to thought, Amy poured the contents of the pot into the large vase. "Whew. Filled it right up." With satisfaction, Amy plunked the pot back on the tray and placed the cup beside it. She'll think you drunk it all."

Amy stroked her cat. "Do you think she'll be all right?"

Lying back against the pillows, Deena surveyed the cat. "I think so. She just needs to sleep it off. . .but Amy, let's keep this a secret. All right?"

Amy studied her with an understanding far beyond her tender years. "I won't tell, Mama." She cradled Gray Lady in her arms. "I don't want you to sleep all the time, either."

The girl is too quick-witted, Deena thought, her head pounding with bone weary tiredness. Her eyes began to close. "A. . .my. I must sleep. . .now. . .get. . .Esie. . ."

Fear quickened Amy's eyes. Deena smiled drowsy reassurance. "I'm all right. . .just tired."

Timidly, Amy patted her mother's shoulder. "Go to sleep then, Mama. May I come back later?"

As Deena nodded, Amy ran to get Esie.

"What is the meaning of this, Kyle? I don't understand why you would do this to me." Helen sucked in a sob. "Your. . . Deena needs constant care. I. . .I just can't do it alone. I *need* Mrs. Bitley."

Shifting onto his other foot, Kyle opened his mouth to acquiesce to Helen's reasonable-sounding demand, only to clamp it shut again. What was he doing? Deena had also made a reasonable request.

Kyle placed his hands on Helen's shoulders. "Esie is eager to be of assistance, and you must admit, she is well qualified. Besides, it makes Deena feel better to have Esie about."

"But your poor wife is nigh out of her head, Kyle. She knows naught what is best." As Helen melted against him, Kyle stepped back.

"My wife was remarkably clearheaded when I saw her."

She brushed his arm. "As you wish, Kyle. Umm. I must

return to the sickroom. As for luncheon. . ." He got the impression she expected an invitation to dine with him. A frown crossed her face when he made no move to do so.

"Enjoy your luncheon, and stop worrying about your child wife," she told him. "I don't need you sick as well."

"She is not a child," Stern repeated.

Helen smiled her apology. "Don't worry, Kyle. I'll do all I can for the poor dear."

Bleakly, Kyle watched her go.

❧

Hours later, Deena awoke clearheaded with Isaiah 41:10 running through her mind: "Fear thou not, for I am with thee: be not dismayed; for I am thy God: I will strengthen thee; yea, I will help thee; yea, I will uphold thee with the right hand of my righteousness."

Deena heard Helen coax the housekeeper. "Esie, take a break. I've almost got this drink ready for Mrs. Stern. I'll see to it while you bring me some luncheon."

Sensing the housekeeper's hesitation, Deena croaked, "Esie, water." Esie hurried to her side.

"Mrs. Stern!" She went to pour water, only to have Helen shove the mug of tea into her hands.

Esie held it to Deena's lips. Though she struggled, some slipped down her throat. As Esie set it aside, Deena whispered. "Please, Esie, water. . .just water."

Helen admonished her. "If you're to get better, you require nourishing liquids. Now. . ."

Deena ignored her. "Esie. . .please. . .water." Lips tight, Esie did as bid and held it for Deena, who drank deeply. "Thank you, Esie."

"If you're hungry, I'll bring luncheon." At Deena's nod, she patted her shoulder. "Good. I'll return straightway." This she addressed to Helen as well as Deena.

After Esie left, Helen held out the tea. "Finish this and I'll get you more."

Deena managed a weak smile. "Not now." She forced herself to meet the other woman's gaze.

"Well then, later, with luncheon." Leaning over, Helen straightened the covers around Deena. Her efforts only made Deena more uncomfortable.

"I'm getting well, Helen." Deena tested her response.

Moving away, Helen stared out the window, her hands clenched tightly at her side. "So it seems. You are proving much stronger than Lizzy." It didn't sound like a compliment.

She reviewed her suspicions in her mind. Even to her they sounded farfetched. Someone meant her harm. Was it Helen? That seemed almost too easy. Then there was Mrs. Bitley. She well knew how to get in and out of Three Oaks, without detection should she so desire, and Helen trusted the woman. What about a disgruntled servant? The possibilities overwhelmed her. One suspect she refused to consider. . .Kyle.

Before Esie returned with a tray, Deena felt herself growing weak, her sight blurry. Still and all it was not as bad as usual. Deena suspected the water had diluted the tea, even as it had for Gray Lady. The thought gave her hope.

In the distance she thought she heard a soft, "Won't work, you know. You cannot fight me, Deena. Not forever."

Then Helen was beside her, all solicitude as Esie bustled over with a tray. Taking the tray, she permitted Esie to help Deena sit up against her pillows. With goodwill, Deena ate the heavy broth and drank the thick milk, thinking the food, too, would offset the poison. Besides, she needed strength.

To her consternation, after the tray had been taken from her, her weakness intensified. The room began to spin sickeningly, her vision blurred. The food! Crying out, Deena tried to escape vague, monstrous arms reaching out to crush her.

"Help me!" she cried again and again as she threw herself about on the bed.

Perplexed, Dr. Meyer tugged his ear. "You say," he addressed the distraught housekeeper, "she was fine at luncheon? This makes no sense."

He glanced at Stern's anxious face. "I don't know what to say. It's a matter for the Lord now."

Kyle left the room, his shoulders hunched. Was there nothing he could do? "Lord God, don't take her from me. Please don't take her from me." Her sweet, innocent face floated before him.

The next afternoon his mood had not lightened. Deena was no better. Helen's face showed the strain of staying awake throughout the night.

She found Stern in the sitting room, staring at the wall. "Kyle. Dearest Kyle. I did so hope she was getting better." Sobbing, she moved into his arms.

"How is she?" he asked dully.

"Very weak. I am so afraid for her, darling."

Stern's arms dropped to his side. Helen touched his enigmatic face. " 'Tis so difficult to watch you suffer. You do love her, don't you, Kyle?" She led him to the sofa, but Kyle scarcely noticed.

But then, she didn't know about the letter Bailey had handed him a few minutes earlier.

Taking the letter, Stern retired to his study. Hesitating but a moment, he slit it open and pulled out not only a long letter from Deena's solicitor, but also a faded document. Curiously, he looked at the birth certificate, then looked again. Groaning, he read the letter.

My lady,
   Enclosed is the proof you requested. I hope it is of assistance to you in quelling rumors. Margaret and I send our felicitations on your nuptials, and pray for the happiness you so deserve. . . .

The letter dropped from Kyle's hand as he sunk into his chair, his head in his hands. Deena was a woman grown and he had denied her the right to truly be his wife. In truth, it wasn't age and vulnerability that kept him from her, but also his own stubborn pride and his unforgiveness toward Lizzy.

Recognizing Deena's accusations as truth, Stern bowed in prayer. "Lord, forgive me!" He loved her! Mayhap he had no right to want her back, but he begged for her life anyway. As for possibility of insanity. . .he couldn't believe it. He wouldn't!

Thinking of the reception, but five days hence, he sighed heavily.

"Ma'am, you be awake." Deena smiled drowsily at the plump housekeeper's obvious relief.

"Good. Give her this." Helen plunked a mug into Esie's hand. The pungent odor brought Deena more fully awake.

"No. . .water," she whispered, nodding from the mug to the vase of flowers on the bed table and back again. Esie stared at her, at the mug, at the vase.

"Drugged," she mouthed. Esie's eyes widened. She glanced over toward Helen's turned back as she carefully poured out the tea and rinsed the mug. By the time Helen turned about, Deena was drinking thirstily from the mug. Only Deena knew Esie had refilled it with water from the jug beside the flowers on the table.

Helen watched. "All gone, good." She began to say more, but gave forth a shrill scream as Amy hopped into the room carrying Gray Lady. Hunching her back, the cat hissed at Helen.

"Get rid of that cat."

Amy stared at her belligerently. "Papa said I could visit Mama whenever I wished, and bring Gray Lady."

Flushed, Helen hurried from the room. "No good will come of this."

"For whom?" muttered Esie as the door closed.

Amy moved cautiously toward the bed. "Are you all right, Mama? Mrs. Billings says sometimes you've an attic to let."

Esie protested, "Stuff and feathers, child. Don't you let that woman bad-mouth your Mama. See, your Mama is tired and weak, but otherwise fine."

Deena ached to reassure her daughter. "If you. . .two will help. . .me, I. . .*will* be all right."

Releasing the cat, Amy ventured to sit on the bed. "Help, I'll help. How?"

"Amy, I want you to join me at mealtimes. Would. . .you like that?" Feeling weak, Deena enunciated her words slowly.

Amy bounced up and down. "Yes, Mama. Could I read to

you too?"

Gray Lady puttered about the bed. Finally, with a satisfied purr, she settled down beside Deena to sleep. Deena touched her softly. Weakness dragged at her limbs.

"Esie, when you bring my tray, see no one has access to it but yourself."

Esie glanced toward Amy. "You suspect *her?*"

Amy piped up. "Something was wrong with the tea. I gave some to Gray Lady and it made her sleep strange for a long time." She clapped her hand over her mouth. "Oh, Mama. I forgot. I haven't told anyone else, truly I haven't."

Deena smiled drowsily. She was losing the battle with fatigue. " 'Tis all right. We can trust Esie."

"You may indeed. I'll see to things." Esie busied herself straightening, cleaning, expending her anger while Amy chatted with her mother until Deena drifted to sleep.

Deena awoke later, but felt no better for the sleep. She found it difficult to focus her mind and wondered if she'd been slipped poison her while she slept.

Seeing Deena was awake, Esie came over to fluff up her pillows behind her back. She was surprised to see the cat still asleep beside her.

"You have not been asleep long, ma'am." The housekeeper turned to Amy. "She's awake again. Why don't you run get your father?"

As Amy reached for her cat, Esie stayed her hand. "Leave be. If you happen to see Mrs. Billings, tell her you left the cat here while you went to get your father." Grinning, Amy patted the cat before dashing from the room.

Esie gave Deena water. "You gonna tell Mr. Stern?"

Deena sighed. "What do I tell him?"

Esie shook her head. "That woman is dangerous. Never did take ta her being here all the time. Not proper, not proper at all."

"I know you want to get rid of her, Esie, but she's been kind to nurse me. But Mrs. Bitley. . ." Her words trailed off as Kyle strode into the room.

Deena felt his shock at her appearance. Yet he smiled as he sat down and took her thin hand in his. "You're awake."

Deena smiled weakly; the nap had done little to strengthen her. If she was to explain, she must needs hurry before once more slipping off to sleep.

Even as she opened her mouth, Stern stroked her cheek. "Helen must be happy to see you improved. Just a short while ago, she was crying, thinking she had failed to help you."

He hurried on. "You received a letter from your lawyer friend, Orrin."

Stern rightly interpreted the question in her eyes. "Yes, he sent it, and I owe you another apology." His grip on her hand tightened. "It wasn't your age which bothered me. I guess, deep down, I believed you about that."

He paused. "You were right. It was Lizzy, rather my refusal to deal with my hurt and bitterness which was the real problem, the real reason I couldn't trust you. But I've asked Jesus to help me forgive Lizzy. I'm ready to put the past where it belongs, in the past."

"I'm glad," whispered Deena. "Yes, I forgive you as well."

Deena stared at the cat waking up from her nap, stretching and clawing slightly at the quilt. "Amy should have taken the cat with her." Stern frowned. "Helen won't return as long as it stays."

Deena gazed at the man who held her heart, her lips sealed. He would not believe her, she knew that now. However badly he felt about doubting her before, if she told him someone was trying to poison her. . .

She winced. Had it not been for Gray Lady, she wouldn't have believed it herself. She needed to find *who* first, needed proof. It seemed so hopeless.

Weakness slipped through her; it took so much effort to stay awake.

"I'm tired," she murmured, not wanting Stern to see her tears.

"I see." Awkwardly, he patted her shoulder, "I'll keep praying for you. I want you well, and not just for Amy." He looked at her a long moment before leaving. Did she read hurt in his eyes?

Tears trickled down Deena's cheeks as the door closed. Esie's arms surrounded her, letting her weep. "I couldn't tell him. I couldn't. He'd think me mad."

"I know, dear. We must discover the truth while still protecting you. If we let on, she'll just think of some other way to hurt you."

Deena shook her head. "We have no proof it's Helen, but we have to make certain I don't ingest anymore of that debilitating drug."

Esie released her, settled her under the covers. "Of course it's Miz Billings. Look what happened with Nellie."

"Helen had nothing to do with that," countered Deena. "That was Mrs. Bitley's doing."

For a moment, animosity twisted the face of the housekeeper. "And Miz Billings got her the job."

She hushed as Helen made her entrance. "Why, Deena, dear, I hear you're doing much better." She smiled, but her eyes were sharp as they beheld the slight figure on the bed. Deena need not fake her exhaustion.

Suddenly Helen stiffened. "That cat! Get that mangy thing out of here!"

Grinning, Esie picked up the cat. "I'll take her ta Amy." She glanced toward Helen. "Madam has already taken nourishment. I just don't understand why she seems so weak."

Deena feigned sleep as Esie departed with Gray Lady.

Sensing Helen near the bed, Deena tensed as she purred, "Poor Kyle." It was the sound Deena heard the night she imagined that Helen tried to push her from the balcony. Esie was right. It *was* Helen. What she felt had been more than jealousy.

Sweat beaded on Deena's forehead from her effort to lie still. Fear churned inside her, chilling her despite the warmth in the room. Sleep came, but no peace.

Nightmares, haunted laughter chased her down the darkened corridors of her mind.

sixteen

"Mrs. Stern." Esie patted Deena's cheek. "Wake up now. She's gone for awhile."

Deena opened her eyes. "Gone. However did you manage?" She watched as Esie dumped the tea and refilled the mug with water. Deena managed to hold a shaking hand to steady the mug. Ever since yesterday when they had foiled attempts to poison her, Deena had been improving. The weakness and leadlike weight of her arms was receding, if slowly. She was learning patience.

She still trembled from the effects of the drug given her during the night, but even that, thanks to Esie's foresight, had been diluted, so its effects had not been as horrific nor as long lasting.

Almost reluctantly, Helen allowed Esie to take over more and more of her duties.

Upstairs, Deena clenched her teeth as she forced her hand inch by inch across the coverlet. Taking a deep breath, she tried to hold the mug all by herself.

Finishing, Deena lay back against the pillows, panting. Her hand dropped limply to the bed. "Ya be acomin' along," Esie said briskly, but Deena saw moisture in her eyes.

"But will it be enough?" Deena spoke with less hesitation.

"Enough?"

"Right, enough. I have an idea how to stop this once and for all, but I have to attend the reception."

The housekeeper's face twisted with concern. " 'Tis Saturday!"

"Esie, I must confront her." Deena's face crumbled. "She hates me so much."

"She be evil itself. Why cain't the master see it?"

"I didn't." Deena's lips tightened. She must expose the

truth for all their sakes.

"Mama!" Amy ran into the room, letting the door slam closed behind her. As she stood beside the bed, Gray Lady leaped from the girl's shoulder onto the bed, turned several times, and settled down for a nap.

Biting her lip with concentration, Deena gently stroked the cat. Amy clapped her hands. "You're better. Can you get up?"

Deena smiled at the girl's enthusiasm. Esie lay a hand on Amy's shoulder. "Not yet, Miss Amy. We have to be patient."

Amy hugged her mother. "Papa will be so glad to hear you can go to the reception. He's been such a grump lately."

Deena exchanged a glance with Esie. "Listen, Amy. I'd like to surprise your father. Will you keep my secret?"

Amy hugged herself. "I *love* secrets."

During luncheon, Esie stood beside the bed, deftly assisting Deena. Time and again Deena blinked away tears of frustration at fumbling with the simple task of bringing a spoonful of broth to her lips. Still and all, Deena felt a sense of exhilaration that she did more than the day before.

Much later, however, when Helen returned with Kyle beside her, Deena lay listlessly against her pillows. The woe-begone look in Kyle's eyes almost made her explain. Only the intense look on Helen's face stayed her.

"And how are we this afternoon?" asked Helen. Deena moved her head slightly.

Frowning, Kyle gingerly sat down on the edge of the bed. "Does this hurt you?" Deena shook her head slightly as Kyle took the hand she made lay limp and weak in his.

"You must get well, darling. Please get well for the reception." Kyle said the same words so often. Were they the least effective? Even as he wondered, Deena's strength faded.

Kyle was at a loss to soothe the fright from her eyes as she lost her tenuous hold on consciousness. Her large eyes closed and once more she slept.

Deena's weakness frightened Kyle. He left filled with despair. Dr. Meyer held out little hope of recovery.

After the doctor departed, the mask Stern kept so carefully

in place crumpled. Sitting down at his desk, he put his head in his hands as he had done not so long before. His shoulders slumped. For a long time he begged God for Deena's life, for another chance for them.

"I love her, Lord. Oh, how I love her. I need her. Amy needs her." He continued in the same vein until a quietness stole over him. No voice spoke, no prophecy came, just a quiet conviction that there was more to come and he must be strong. . .strong for Deena.

He looked in on her once more before retiring for the night. Deena slept peacefully, her silver hair streaming over the pillows. So lovely, so frail. "She looks so. . .insubstantial," Kyle murmured sadly, gently stroking Deena's soft cheek. "I wonder at times if she'll just fade away."

"Oh, Kyle," Helen murmured, leaning against his broad chest. His arm encircled her absently as he stared down at his sleeping wife. As he lay his chin on Helen's head, she snuggled closer, then clenched her fists as he murmured dully, "Oh, Helen, I love her so much. I didn't think it possible to love as I love her. . .nor will I again. I can't bear to lose her."

"Kyle, I know."

But something in her tone made Kyle glance at her sharply. For a moment he would have sworn he saw fury in her eyes, then Helen smiled, convincing him he had imagined it.

"Go on to bed, Kyle. There is naught you can do here."

Gazing at his wife one last time, Kyle went to his room. Whatever happened, Deena would always be an angel sent to break through the cold shell about his heart and help him not only to forgive, but to love again.

In her nightmares, Deena heard a voice, "It's time for this to end. What better time than during the reception."

When Deena awoke, she gulped down cool liquid. Her eyes caught those of Esie, who nodded her assurance that the liquid was untainted.

"Oh," she moaned. "Leave me be, Esie. I'm so weak. So tired. Please, the nightmares. Go away." She feigned restless sleep.

"She'll be like that the rest of the night," Helen said. "You might as well go to your quarters, there's nothing more for either of us to do this night." Reluctantly, Esie acquiesced.

Deena awoke late, but bright and alert. She even grimaced at Helen's turned back, but lay still as Helen and Esie changed her sheets. It was so difficult to lie still when for the first time in weeks, her body tingled with life. She wanted to move, to walk, to dance! How silly. She could not dance with her leg. She smothered her chuckle in a cough.

Under Helen's nose, Esie switched the tea for not water, but milk she smuggled up from the kitchen. Drinking it too quickly, Deena choked. Concerned, Esie patted her back. "You all right, ma'am?"

Helen moved up behind the plump housekeeper, watching sharply. Deena's gaze dulled, she slurred, "Seems. . .different today. . .stronger?"

Helen blanched, recovered. "Drink it all."

Esie held the cup so Helen could not see the milky contents. "Miz Billings be right, ma'am. This will make you strong. Now, drink up." Esie was all humility. Deena would have grinned if it were not all so serious.

"Just what she needs, right, Mrs. Billings?" Esie kept hold of the cup.

Helen positively beamed at the woman. "Yes, yes, of course, Esie. You just give her as much of that as possible."

Deena sensed she saw Esie as a scapegoat, should she need one. The thought infuriated her and she fisted her hands beneath the covers.

"How do you feel today?" Helen asked.

Slowly, Deena moved her head to one side. "Better," she whispered, then closed her eyes as if speaking exhausted her. From lowered lashes, she saw the gleam in Helen's eyes. How dare she betray Kyle's trust!

Anger boiled over as she opened her eyes. Accusations trembled on her lips. Reading her correctly, Esie lay a hand on her arm. The warning came through clearly. Turning her head, Deena closed her eyes.

Lord, help me know the truth! Almost she had endangered herself, and the future of the two people she loved most in this world, not to mention the future of the servants who had shown her such care. Her anger dissipated abruptly.

Amy was a welcome interruption to her dark thoughts. She followed a maid with a breakfast tray. The maid nervously handed the tray over to Esie, as Amy and Gray Lady perched on the bed.

Helen shook her head, "I see not why you must breakfast here. You certainly don't think your mother can eat such things. Well, no matter. I'll see if Mr. Stern is downstairs in the breakfast room."

Esie set the tray in front of Deena; buttered a piece of toast, and held it out for her mistress. Determinedly, Deena took the bread. Her arms felt stronger today. Nevertheless, the meal she shared with her daughter, while giving her a sense of well-being, tired her out considerably. At one point, Deena carefully tore off a piece of bacon and threw it to the cat on the rug beside the bed. The little cat pounced on the bacon as though it were alive, then retreated under a nearby chair to eat in solitude.

Deena laughed along with her daughter. "Oh, Mama, you're so much better."

"I don't recall being so hungry for a long time," Deena commented, finishing up the scrambled eggs and draining the glass of milk.

"We'll see you get larger portions," promised Esie.

"Won't that make Mrs. Billings suspicious?" Deena asked.

Esie surveyed her. "Good, you're finally convinced. She had no business being at Three Oaks, her an' her high-flown airs. She brought Mrs. Bitley here and my baby—"

Amy interrupted Esie's tirade. "I'll say how hungry I am." She eyed her mother. " 'Tis true enough. Cook says I'm always hungry."

Deena laughed. "I see I'm in good hands."

Amy wrapped her arms around her mother's neck. "I'll take good care of you, Mama."

Deena's eyes misted as her arms held Amy for the first

time in weeks. "How can I help but recover with such attention from my favorite little girl. . .my daughter."

The arms about her neck tightened. "I love you, Mama." Releasing her, Amy sat back. "God is good, Mama. He answered my prayer. I told Him if He took you away I wouldn't love Him anymore. He can't be a good God and take you away."

"Oh, Amy. God loves us so very much. Sometimes we do bad things or bad things happen to us. but that doesn't mean God doesn't love us. He is still there even if He doesn't stop all the evil in the world." Even to Deena her explanation sounded inadequate. Perhaps God had answered Amy's prayer, and her own.

By midafternoon Deena slyly began flexing her legs beneath the covers. It felt good to be in control of her body once more, and it became more and more difficult to pretend weakness whenever Helen hovered near. Thankfully, as Deena appeared to weaken, Helen took longer and longer breaks.

Late that afternoon, Kyle stepped in to see his wife. She lay before him, scarcely able to keep her eyes open. She feigned sleep, hating herself for her deception. His sadness and despair washed over her. She willed herself not to sit up and cry, "Kyle, Kyle. It's all right. I'm going to be all right."

Kyle stared down at his wife. "She isn't getting any better, is she? Helen, what am I to do? I suppose it's too late to cancel the reception."

Helen smiled up at him as she leaned against him. "Dearest Kyle, don't you think your dear little wife would wish you to go ahead?"

"How can I play host when she lies here like this? I want to be with her. And what will I tell the guests?"

Helen's eyes flashed sympathy. "That the reception is in her honor."

The next morning, after surveying Deena's pale face, Helen sighed and went off riding with Kyle. "She is not better, then," Kyle said. It was not a question and Helen did not try to answer.

Kyle lapsed into silence, not noticing the pains she had taken to fashion her hair under the stylish black riding hat, nor the perfect cut of her gold-trimmed riding jacket and skirt. His only thought was that black did not set off Helen's coloring to advantage as it did his Deena.

The very thought of Deena lying helpless while Helen rode beside him filled him with an inexplicable anger.

Meanwhile, in Deena's chamber, Amy and her mother polished off a rather substantial breakfast. After Esie handed off the breakfast tray to the middle-aged maid, Esie locked the door. Efficiently, Esie helped Deena into a long, soft white robe.

Pulling back the covers, Esie moved Deena's legs over the side of the bed and helped her sit up.

"Mama, are you dizzy?"

"A mite." She was glad of Esie's strong arm around her shoulders. Her smile at Amy wobbled at the dull thud of pain in her forehead. Deena waited impatiently for the room to stop spinning. "It's. . .it's all right now." She sucked in a deep breath. "I want to stand."

"It's too soon, ma'am."

"No, Esie. I must try now." She hung onto Esie as the disapproving housekeeper slid her gently to the floor. Even the slight thud of her feet on the rug sent shock waves of pain up Deena's wasted limbs.

The groan that escaped her clenched teeth worried Amy. "Mama, are you all right?"

"Umm." Deena tried to assure the girl, her face white with the strain. Swaying, she leaned hard into Esie's comforting bulk.

"Enough for now, ma' am."

"No, no time." Deena grunted. She tried to step forward as the pain eased somewhat, but her bad leg refused to hold her. Exhausted, she permitted Esie to tuck her back into bed.

Deena smiled tiredly into her daughter's anxious face. "I stood at least, didn't I?"

" 'Twill go better next time, Mama. I know it will." Amy hugged her mother.

Deena managed to keep up her front until the girl left, taking the cat with her. Then tears of frustration slipped down her cheeks. "I have to walk, Esie, the reception is tomorrow eve!"

Exhausted and upset, Deena fell into a deep, restless slumber. Nightmares haunted her. Helen, like a demonic being, hovered over her paralyzed form, her lovely countenance distorted in the very embodiment of evil. "No!" She came out of her nightmare with a jerk to find herself held fast in Kyle's arms.

"Deena, darling." Warmed in the arms of her husband, she drew on his strength.

Not seeing the desperate look on his face, she did not know his panic as he followed Helen into the room only to find her crying out. Impulsively, he leaped to her side and pulled her into her arms.

Deena, witnessing the reality of her dream in Helen's face, hid her face against Kyle's broad shoulder. She knew the comfort of Kyle's arms would cost her dearly.

"Kyle," she whispered. She wanted to beg him to stay, beg him to rid her of Helen's presence. But she couldn't accuse without proof. She'd have to trust God to keep her safe until then.

"Darling," Kyle murmured, brushing a kiss against her hair.

Helen broke. "Kyle, upon my word, the child is extremely ill. You must not maul her so."

Reluctantly, Kyle released her, lay her gently back against her pillows. Unable to keep the love from her eyes, Deena smiled at him. "Thank you, Kyle."

"Deena." His voice failed him.

Curiosity made her ask. "How. . .is. . .Princess?" She purposefully mumbled.

"She's fine. Sure misses you." He spoke of Princess and other horses for some time until Helen hustled him from the room. Chuckling at her exasperation, Kyle kissed Deena before going to change from his riding clothes.

After his departure, Helen poured out tea and had it to

Deena's lips before Esie returned, breathing heavily from climbing the stairs so quickly. Seeing the fear in Deena's eyes, she hurried to the bed.

"Let me take that, ma'am. Wouldn't want ta stain that lovely habit." Helen gave over.

Esie chatted as she pretended to give Deena the tea. "Sarah be up shortly with luncheon. Amy's anxious to share it with her mama." She smiled. "Cook is grateful you fix the tea yourself. Leastwise she doesn't have that worry."

Helen chuckled. "My pleasure. Least I can do." She entered the small dressing room off the bedchamber to arrange her hair.

Helen came out to find the pot noticeably lower. "She drunk two mugs," said Esie, not adding 'twas water, not tea, Deena drank. The housekeeper shook her head. "She's very weak."

"Mayhap then Amy should skip luncheon with her mother."

Too late. Behind Sarah, carrying a large tray, Amy entered the room with Gray Lady in her arms. Leaping from the girl's arms, the cat skidded to a stop at Helen's feet, hair raised, spitting and clawing. With a cry, Helen fled the room.

While Amy and her mother heartily partook of the sumptuous roast venison, potatoes, greens, apple cobbler with fresh cream (some of which Amy poured out for Gray Lady), and cider, Esie slipped downstairs to refill the teapot with fresh, fragrant tea.

"There," she said, wiping her hands on her white apron. She poured it out with great ceremony. "Your tea, ma'am."

Raising her head haughtily, Deena sipped the tea. "Oh, quite up to snuff."

Touching Deena's cheeks, Esie commented, " 'Tis good to hear you laugh, ma'am. Getting too much color in those cheeks, though. Umm." Esie went into the dressing room where Helen kept her things. She came back with the white powder Helen kept to disguise the lines in her face.

After a quick dusting, Esie surveyed her work. "Now you look ready to depart this world." By the time she returned from the dressing room, Deena had already thrown back the covers and had her legs over the side.

"Ma'am!" Esie hurried over with a warm robe and helped Deena stand.

This time the dizziness faded quickly and Deena was able to shuffle forward with Esie supporting her on one side, and Amy on the other. While unable to still a groan or two, Deena managed to make it across the room and back before collapsing on the bed.

Amy clapped her hands. "Mama, you did it! You walked!" Flinging herself into her mother's arms, Amy burst into tears. "You're going to be all right."

Deena patted the girl's back. "Yes, Amy. . .and you helped." This dried the girl's tears. "Amy, would you mind if I took a nap now?"

"Sure, Mama. I'll return later." Even as Amy picked up her cat and hopped from the room, Deena slept.

Later in the afternoon, she accepted tea from Helen, knowing Esie had refilled the pot. She drank it greedily. Moments later, as the room began to blur, she knew she had made a dreadful mistake. Esie had made the tea. Esie, who always had access to the food. Esie, who'd do almost anything to get rid of Helen. Esie. . .her friend.

"No!" She cried out as colors and patterns wove together frighteningly. Her head pounded, her strength slipped away. "NO! NO!"

seventeen

Deena's restless cries frightened Amy, who came in to share the meal with her mother. "Mama,'" she wailed. "Mama!"

Esie pulled the little girl to her ample bosom. "You best go, Miss Amy. Trust me, I'll see ta your mama."

With frightened eyes, the little girl scooted from the room, clutching Gray Lady so tightly the cat meowed in protest. She almost collided with the doctor, who entered the room with Stern.

"Oh, Dr. Meyer," Helen moaned as the doctor frowned. "Mrs. Stern seems to have taken a turn for the worse."

"Precisely when did this occur?" the doctor snapped, checking Deena's irregular pulse and feeling her heated forehead.

"Mayhap an hour past or so." Helen shrugged helplessly. "The poor child just began screaming, and acting, well, rather addlepated."

"My wife," Kyle corrected Helen firmly.

The doctor's frown deepened as he bent to examine his patient. " 'Tis almost as though. . ." He hesitated, straightened to look at Helen. "What had she to eat before this happened?"

Helen's eyes widened. "Let's see. Oh, yes, tea. She had tea with dear little Amy. She may have consumed some of the sandwiches and sweets sent up. Right, Esie?"

Esie's lips tightened. " 'Tis a fact. I give the tea *Miz Billings* brews fer her."

Helen eyed Esie suspiciously. "A simple herbal recipe, doctor. Drink it myself. Question is, what can we do now?"

Suspicion also lurked in the doctor's eyes as he looked from one woman to the other. "I suggest liquids, lots of liquids to flush out her system. Her symptoms are so like that of her sister, almost as though. . . Esie, didn't you also help with Mrs. Stern's sister?"

"When needed," admitted the housekeeper grudgingly.

He surveyed Stern, bowed with grief. "Sorry," he sighed, his shoulders sagged. "I fear only a miracle will bring her back now."

"Oh, Dr. Meyer," Helen moaned. Esie thrust her clenched fists into the large pockets of her apron.

Leaning over the bed, Kyle stroked Deena's pale cheek. "Deena, my love," he murmured. Turning, he slowly followed the doctor from the room, his face white with raging self-condemnation.

As the door closed, Helen stared at the housekeeper. "If it helps, I trust you."

"Ma'am," said Esie. "There be nothin' more you can do fer the poor thing. Let me have a room made up fer you. I can spend the night here." She shrugged with deliberation. " 'Tis only a matter of waiting now."

Helen eyed the woman through narrowed, thoughtful eyes. "I suppose you're right, Esie."

Walking to the mirror, Helen traced the spidery lines about her eyes and mouth. "I have been losing far too much sleep. Indeed, I do need to rest if I am to be presentable."

Helen paused at the door. "If by chance, Deena comes about, notify me immediately." She tried, and failed, to look concerned. "I must not neglect my duties to my patient."

"You be asayin' I don't be adoin' my job?" Esie put her hands on her hips. "Mayhap it be jest as well then, you sit with Mrs. Stern during her last tortured hours."

Helen shuddered. "No, no, Esie, that's all right. But. . .you will call."

Esie waited until Helen's footsteps echoed down the hall before turning toward the bed. With an efficiently and agility belying her size, Esie raced to the kitchen and brought up a can of hot water, some of which she poured into a basin.

Gently Esie bathed her mistress, and changed not only her nightgown, but the bedding. Finally, she tucked up the fresh warm covers about Deena's neck.

There was water enough left to clean the tea kettle and refill it. Briskly, Esie thoroughly washed out the cup. Throughout the long night, she forced liquid into her restless, resistant mistress. Sometimes she managed only a few drops at a time, rubbing Deena's throat to make her swallow.

Toward morning, Deena gave a long, drawn-out sigh and fell into a deep, natural sleep. Sighing, Esie set down the cup, her arm aching from exhaustion. Tiredly, she stumbled into the comfortable chair pulled up next to the bed.

Esie awoke with a start. Had she imagined the slight movement from the bed? Shoving herself to her feet, Esie stared down at her mistress. "Yer awake!"

Fear chilled Deena. "You. . .you drugged. . ."

Esie said. "She be sure of herself now. Mustn't in anywise catch you conscious."

Deena shook her head. "Not. . .Helen. . .you."

Esie's eyes widened. "No. Never! You saved my baby. I'd never hurt you." Her distress was unmistakable.

Noticing the heavy lines about Esie's eyes, she asked, "What happened?"

"It was in the cup, but don't you worry. I'm not about to let that harridan win."

"I'm sorry."

Esie patted her shoulder. "I understand."

This time Deena actually managed a smile. "Thirsty."

She drank deeply as Esie held the cup. Deena sighed as Esie lay her head back against the pillows. 'Twas good to be in control of her faculties once more.

Hearing the door open, Deena fastened her eyes shut until she heard the hesitant footsteps heading her way. Esie shielded Deena from view, and it was to her Amy spoke. "Mrs. Billings says not to come up. She says Mama," Amy choked, continued with difficulty. "She said Mama's going to die."

Finger to her lips, Esie moved aside so Amy could see Deena. The little girl's eyes widened. "Amy."

"Oh, Mama. You're alive!"

Esie touched the girl's shoulder. "Been touch and go, Miss Amy, but I think she's through the worst of it. But, 'tis important Mrs. Billings not know what we know. No one must know, understand?"

Amy nodded. "I won't tell, promise."

"Good, because I'm going to need your help tonight."

"Will it help, Mama?"

"It will, but no one must know what we're about, certainly not Mrs. Billings."

" 'Cause she wants Mama to die."

Esie hesitated. "We must see to it she does not ever hurt your mother again. Now, do you think you can bring your mother some milk and something to eat without raising anyone's suspicions?"

Amy grinned conspiratorially. "I'll just beg food from Cook. I'm always asking for Gray Lady." She reached for the cat, which had leaped from her shoulder to the bed, then stopped. "Best I leave her here, right?"

Not long hence, Amy returned carrying a tray holding two bowls. One contained stew, the other milk. Deena's eyes sparkled amusement as Amy set the tray before her.

With a wry smile, Amy defended herself. "Well, Cook did think it for Gray Lady."

In a thrice, Esie had the milk poured into the cup and held it for Deena. Before Deena fell asleep, Esie managed to get most of the stew down her too.

Hearing the door open, Esie whisked the tray from the bed while Amy grabbed the bowls and set them down for the eager cat. As Helen marched full into the room, Gray Lady was busily licking the last dregs of stew from the bowl.

"I heard you had come up here with a tray, Amy." Then she took in the cat and shuddered. "Must you feed that mangy animal up here?"

Shrugging, Amy picked up the bowls and replaced them on the tray. Gray Lady protested loudly. "Guess she wants more," said Amy. After setting the cat on her shoulder, she picked up the tray.

Esie shook her head to silence any ill-advised word about their plans for later that evening. Amy merely grinned at her from behind Helen's back.

Helen almost caught the exchange as she turned. "Amy, you needn't bother coming up here again. Your mother doesn't know you anymore."

Amy's grin hardened into a cold hard stare reminiscent of her father. "She's *my* mama. I shall see her when I choose to see her. And," she added defiantly, "*you* can't stop me!" She let the door slam shut behind her.

"'Well, I never!" exclaimed Helen.

Lowering her eyes, Esie busied herself cleaning out the cup which so recently held nourishing stew and milk.

"I suppose," Helen commented, "you cleaned out the teapot as well."

"Yes, ma'am. I try ta please."

"I wish I still had Mrs. Bitley," Helen muttered, adding, "Has she shown any signs of awakening?"

Esie sighed heavily. "She jest sleeps and sleeps and sleeps, like it'll be forever."

"Umm, forever. Poor dear." Helen turned away. Before she left, she had a fresh pot of hot water sent up and brewed a fresh batch of tea. "Get some of this down her if you can."

"Yes, ma'am, I understand perfectly."

Helen glanced suspiciously at the stolid housekeeper; Esie met her gaze until Helen glanced away.

Later, Helen returned with Kyle. Despondently, he stared down at the woman he had come to love too late. Running a caressing hand down Deena's cheek, he whispered, "Oh, Deena. . .my darling Deena." He could say not more for his throat tightened into a hard knot. He did not stay long.

Watched over by Esie, Deena slept most of the day. She did not witness Stern's despair that evening when he visited her before dragging himself off to his chambers to ready himself for the evening.

Stern rued the day he had agreed to go ahead with the reception. Why ever had he allowed Helen to talk him into such a farce? No, the decision had been his. He'd prayed and hoped for Deena's recovery.

He knew how his conservative neighbors would view the situation. Helen playing hostess while his own wife lay dying so mysteriously upstairs. He shuddered at what lay ahead. Jerking his black superfine evening jacket into place, Stern set his face for the looks, the suspicion, the rumors he knew would circulate this night. As though headed for the guillotine, Stern straightened his shoulders and marched from the room.

In the dining hall, his eyes raked over the revealing décolletage of Helen's dramatic gold-and-black gown. For a moment, his eyes lit in appreciation of the brief bodice, then hardened with disgust. "You like it, Kyle?"

"Hardly the proper thing for the guests we expect tonight," he said dryly.

Helen laughed, howbeit uncertainly. "Give the country yokels something to gossip about for months."

"That is not something I care overmuch to encourage, Helen." Stern spoke repressively. "I would have thought, with Deena, my wife, and your patient, I might add, lying helpless upstairs, you might have used better judgment."

The sudden blaze of anger in her eyes surprised him. The next moment, she steered the dinner conversation, what there was of it, away from the immediate concerns of them both. For the first time, Kyle felt uncomfortable in her presence.

Deena scarcely had time to lie down before Helen barged into the bedchamber and tersely dismissed Esie.

Deena sensed Esie's hesitation, but when Helen again barked out her dismissal, Deena heard the housekeeper's reluctant withdrawal. She heard the door open, but not click closed.

Helen paced back and forth, stopping now and again to glower down at Deena. "Soon you shall be but a faint memory and Kyle, dearest Kyle, shall be mine."

Deena shuddered as Helen ripped off the mask she'd worn so well; gone the gracious friend and neighbor.

She chuckled, a terrible, spine-chilling chuckle. "Lizzy could not keep him from me. Even dear Ralph could not keep me from Kyle. As for you, foolish child, you never even had a chance. Stubborn you are, like Lizzy, but, of course, she was weakened by the birthing of my husband's baby. It should have been mine."

Deena stiffened as she stilled a gasp at this revelation. Thankfully, Helen was pacing once again and didn't notice.

Turning, Helen paced back toward the bed. "Ah, yes," she continued calmly as though holding casual conversation, "Kyle never knew his light skirt had taken my husband, his friend, to her bed." She laughed again. "Ah, but I discovered it.

"Yes, I knew. Poor Ralph was besotted with that creature who pretended to be my friend, while behind my back. . ." her voice grated harshly.

"Kyle never knew, never suspected his friend had betrayed him as surely as his profligate wife." Helen laughed again. "But I took care of things. I was not going to let Lizzy bear my husband's baby when I could not. 'Twas simple to help Lizzy down the stairs. Even she was never sure it was more than an accident."

Deena forced herself not to react. *Dear God, the woman's mad. Help me!* She wished the woman would stop her gleeful confession, but Helen continued.

"Just like I," she chuckled, "nursed you, Deena, I nursed dear Lizzy, nursed her to death." She rolled the word tantalizingly on her tongue. "In the end she knew, tried to fight back, but it was too late—much, much too late.

"Then I had to bear the news to Ralph. Devastated him. I let him know I knew his dirty little secret. Lizzy was dead and I was glad." Helen paused.

"Poor Ralph guessed what I had done. He actually threatened to have me committed. Threatened to inform Kyle. Couldn't have that, so Ralph had to die." Her matter-of-fact tone chilled Deena.

Still Helen ranted. "Kyle was there to comfort me. In time he would have asked me to be his wife. . .me. I was content to wait." Spinning toward the bed again, she spat out, "Then you came. You with your innocent ways and that hair."

Growling in anger, Helen pulled out a pair of shears. "Yes,

that hair." Grabbing a handful, she jerked it toward her with such force, Deena groaned. Her response brought forth a harsh laugh from Helen.

At that moment, Esie clamored into the room. "What are you doing back?" Helen demanded shrilly, shoving the shears into a nearby drawer.

"I thought, ma'am," she puffed, "as to how it be gettin' late, ye be wanting ta git yourself smartened up fer the party."

Helen held her anger in check with some difficulty.

"I was going to give Deena some fresh tea before I go."

Esie reached for the cup. "Now, ma'am. 'Tis my place to do that. You go on."

Helen hesitated, then a smile lifted her lips. "You're right, of course. Be sure she takes it all."

"She'll be gettin' all she's supposed to," said Esie firmly.

Satisfied, Helen left the room. Esie turned to get rid of the drugged tea in the pot when Deena stayed her hand. "Stop, Esie, We need that."

"Not to drink!"

"Of course not. We will need it for proof when we confront her."

"Aye, that we do." Esie set it aside carefully.

Pushing herself to a sitting position, Deena waited until the dizziness subsided before inching her legs over the side of the bed.

After Esie was convinced Deena would not fall, she brought out the lovely dress Deena had worn at her wedding. It seemed so long ago. She had been so full of hope. Deena pushed the depressing thought away.

The process of bathing, having her hair washed, dried, and styled as well as dressing greatly sapped Deena's meager strength. Esie had to sew her gaunt mistress into the gown. Esie arranged Deena's wonderful hair high on her head with a cascade of curls falling like a silver waterfall down her back.

Closing her eyes momentarily, Deena murmured the verse from Isaiah that had come to mean so much to her: "Fear thou not; for I am with thee: be not dismayed; for I am thy God:

I will strengthen thee. . . ."

Fear not. That was a hard thing to do in the face of the evil that surrounded her, but wasn't God greater than fear?

Esie's work-roughened fingers clasped Deena's diamond necklace about her neck.

"Now you shall be the belle of the ball."

"There are more important things afoot this night." She exchanged a conspiratorial smile with the housekeeper. "Tonight, Lord willing, Helen's evil scheme comes to an end once and for all."

Esie muttered. "It is about time. Now, where is that child?"

As though on command, Amy rushed into the room, the cat on her shoulder. "Ready, Mama?"

"How are things downstairs?" Deena asked.

"Papa just glares at everyone. Keeps lookin' up at the picture. Then he looks so sad. Mrs. Billings smiles and laughs. She won't leave Papa alone, not that he notices, but," she bit her lip, "some of them are saying mean things about Papa."

Amy reached up to steady the cat. "Mrs. Billings said was time I was abed, so I got Gray Lady and came on up. May I bring her along?"

"Certainly. I would not be here if it were not for Gray Lady." She glanced at Esie. "I'm ready, Esie."

Nodding, the housekeeper helped her mistress to her feet. As they walked to the door, Deena called back. "Oh, Amy, bring that mug of tea. Careful now."

Amy held the mug with both hands. "You gonna make *her* sleep all strange?"

"Well, I do hope to show your father what she tried to do."

"You mean, hurt you. I'll do my part, Mama." She had her father's look.

"Thank you, Amy." On the housekeeper's arm, Deena limped out of the room and down the hallway to the long staircase. Amy followed with the mug.

At the stairs, Deena swayed dizzily, clutched Esie. "Breathe in deep, ma'am."

Deena sucked in deep breaths, waited until her breathing

eased and her dizziness faded. "Now." Slowly, step by step by step, Esie helped her descend to the polished floor. It proved too much for the weakened Deena. She slumped limply against Esie, who lowered her onto the bottom step.

"Mama?" Amy sat down beside her.

"Let her rest a moment, Amy." Esie held Deena's head against her ample bosom. Deena's ragged breath sounded loud in the hall, where all was still except for the distant murmur of voices.

"Are you sure about this, ma'am?"

Deena nodded. She had not exerted herself in so long. "Lord, please give me strength. Give me strength." Her own gone, Deena knew she needed help to force her trembling limbs to do her will. Leaning back, she closed her eyes.

Then, to Esie's amazement, Deena straightened, opened her eyes. "I'm ready now, Esie." She even managed a smile for Amy. "Come. It's time."

A slight smile touched Esie's face as she helped her mistress to her feet. Glancing upward, Deena murmured, "Thank You," as new strength flowed into her limbs. Slowly they made their way to the large doors to the parlor. Bailey's eyes widened at the sight of them.

"Please announce me," Deena commanded. No weakness sounded in her voice.

"With pleasure, ma'am." Opening the doors, he announced, "May I present, Mrs. Kyle Stern."

Laughter died on stunned lips as the guests stared at the diminutive woman walking into the room on the arm of a plump maid.

Deena kept her eyes on her husband's ashen face as she staggered to a stop a pace in front of him. Beside him, Helen clung to his arm in desperation, her eyes wild. "It can't be true. You're dead!"

Stern stepped away from her as though stung. "What did you say?"

White-faced, Helen collected her wits. "Not important, Kyle. Just surprised." She smiled hesitantly at Deena. "Now, dear child, you must return to your chamber immediately. I'll see you get settled in."

Deena looked her in the eye. "Why, so you can murder me as you intended all along?"

Helen gasped. "Kyle, dear, the child is beside herself. We must get her to bed."

Frowning, Kyle reached for his wife. As one, Deena, Esie, and Amy stepped out of reach. "No, Papa. You must listen to Mama."

"I told you to go to bed, young lady." Helen noted the cat. "And get that horrid beast out of here!" She cowered behind Kyle.

"Amy," Kyle's face was unreadable.

"Stop!" Deena commanded. She sagged against Esie, who held her more tightly. "Now, Helen. I just thought you might wish a taste of the tea you fixed for me. Amy." Stepping forward, Amy held out the mug.

"What's this!" demanded Kyle, but Helen cut him off.

"You insolent chit," she cried, smashing the mug to the floor. "How dare you come down here pandering your noddy-cocked fantasies." She glared at Deena, who held her gaze steadily. Neither noticed the cat.

"No!" Amy grabbed for Gray Lady, who leaped from her shoulder to lap up the spilled tea. "No!"

"Amy! Get that cat!" It was Kyle.

"Mama!" The little girl cried, snatching up the cat and holding her in her arms. "Is she gonna go to sleep like last time?"

"What's this?" Kyle thundered. But even as he spoke, the little gray cat stiffened, cried out softly, gasped once, and lay still.

"Lady! Lady!" Amy screamed, clutching the cat.

Deena touched the soft fur. "She's dead, Amy."

Screeching, Amy launched herself at Helen. "You killed my cat! You killed my cat and you tried to kill Mama!"

But for Kyle's quick reflexes, Helen would have fallen. He held her in a viselike grip. "What's this?"

She looked into his cold face and quailed. "Kyle."

Grabbing her, he demanded. "Helen, is this true?"

Helen glared at Deena, whose arms surrounded the weeping child. "You. It's all your fault. You had no right, no right to take what belonged to me."

Kyle's face whitened. He pushed Helen away and reached toward his wife and daughter, bewilderment on his face. "Amy, go with Esie. She'll take care of you." He motioned for a footman to take care of the cat as Esie released Deena into Kyle's waiting arms.

Gently, Esie led Amy from the room. Kyle felt Deena tremble against him. Carefully, he picked her up and sat down with her on a nearby settee.

"Now, what's this all about?" Slowly, painfully, Deena explained. She did not need to look at Stern to know that for the first time he truly listened. "Esie and Amy helped protect me. Helen wanted me to die tonight. She meant to kill me as she did Lizzy and her husband."

Kyle stiffened. "What?'"

"Helen murdered my sister. . .and her own husband."

"But why? Lizzy was her friend." Kyle seem to have forgotten his guests, who listened soundlessly.

Deena looked at her husband sadly. "Lizzy carried her husband's baby."

The shock of betrayal sat heavily on his face. "Lizzy. . .and Ralph?"

Deena nodded. "I'm sorry, Kyle. Helen had no intention of permitting either Lizzy or the baby to live."

"That fall."

"No accident."

"Lizzy knew, at the end. She tried to tell me." Kyle closed his eyes. "She wasn't insane, was she? Helen poisoned her. But Ralph?"

"She taunted him with what she had done. When he threatened to turn her in, she killed him."

Kyle groaned. "When I think of the danger to which I've subjected you. . ."

"You didn't know. She wanted you for herself, Kyle."

"I never gave her cause to think. . . She must be completely addlepated if she thought I'd ask for her hand after you died!" He paused. "She told you all this?"

"She thought I was dying. She didn't know Esie was doing her best to keep what I ate and drank drug-free. It did not work always, but enough."

"Darling, darling Deena, why didn't you tell me? You didn't think I'd believe you, did you?" He was surprised there was no anger in her eyes, only sadness.

"At times, Helen had *me* half convinced I was going mad."

Suddenly Kyle looked around. "Where is that woman? Where is that woman who tried to murder my wife?" The guests stared at each other as though awaking from a nightmare.

"Where is she?" he grated. "She must be apprehended at once."

Questions, murmurs, a shrugged shoulder. "She's gone."

Stern motioned for a footman. "Tell Crooks to find Mrs. Billings and bring her back immediately." The footman inclined his head, but from the gleam in his eyes Stern knew he relished the assignment. Obviously, no one but himself had been fooled by the woman.

Closing her eyes, Deena leaned limply in Kyle's arms. "Dearest love. If only I'd realized."

When she looked up, he saw the truth in her eyes and groaned softly. "I'm sorry. So very sorry." How could she forgive him? He thought of her struggling almost alone against overwhelming evil. How could he not have suspected?

"I do not wish to interrupt." Deena started in Kyle's arms. She stared drowsily into the sympathetic blue eyes of a dignified matron dressed in the first stare of fashion. "I'm sorry. I fear we have greatly mistaken the situation."

Kyle, his lips tight, nodded. Deena gave the woman a warm smile. "Thank you," she said softly. Glancing about the room, she no longer felt censure. Though not warm, the faces toward them were also not condemning. 'Twas a start, at least.

"I should carry you up to your room."

Deena shivered. "Not yet. . .not alone."

Kyle held her close. "No, you're right. I'll not leave you alone."

The guests, loathe to leave until the drama was ended, milled about the large room eating, drinking, and conversing in low voices. Deena slept against Kyle's shoulder.

"Master Stern!" The door to the parlor burst open and Crooks stood before them, breathing heavily. "We found her, Master Stern."

"You have her secure, I trust," Kyle said, ice in his tone.

"In a manner of speakin', sir." He paused to get his breath. "She's dead, sir."

"Dead!"

"Aye, must 'ave been atoolin' mighty smart when a wheel of her gig buckled. Threw her clear. Broke 'er neck, sir. We brought her back. The maids be seein' to her."

There was vindication in his eyes as he left the room with Stern's thanks.

Hastily the guests made their exit, leaving Deena and Kyle alone in the large room. Kyle glanced up at the lovely portrait over the mantel.

"My Deena." His arm tightened about her. "I love you so much, and almost lost you by my unforgiving heart and mistrust."

Deena stared deep into his eyes. "Truly, you love me? I thought you cared for her. You made it clear you married me out of a sense of duty." Deena bit her lip, finally whispered. "You didn't want me as your wife."

"Oh, yes, I did, I do. Helen has never been more than a friend, at least on my part. I want *you* as my wife, *you* as mother of our children."

Tears glistened on her cheeks. "I'm sorry too. I've been so angry with you, I didn't give you much of a chance either." She smiled slightly. "These last days I've had to learn patience. I've seen your pain. Oh, Kyle, I do love you." She blushed.

"Oh, darling." Holding her against his heart, he captured her lips in a kiss full of love and promise.

Snuggling in his arms, Deena knew she'd finally come home.

epilogue

Two years later, a lovely woman greeted the tall woman and her balding husband. "Margaret!" Deena hugged the other woman. "It's so good of you to come. So good to see you. Orrin, you too."

Margaret surveyed her former charge. "You look radiant."

Deena laughed up into the tender face of her husband, who took Orrin's hand. "Glad to make your acquaintance, Mr. Worth. I can only thank you for sending Deena to America. Good to see you again too, Margaret."

"Mama?" A young girl walked into the room carefully carrying a small bundle.

After hugging her daughter, Deena took the bundle and pulled back the blanket to reveal a round face with startling gray eyes. "May I also introduce you to the newest member of our family."

"Oh, he's beautiful!" exclaimed Margaret, holding out her arms to take the child.

Kyle smiled proudly down at his daughter. "This is Amy's very special baby brother, Seth."

Amy blushed; Deena patted her arm. "I don't know what I would do without my daughter."

Margaret smiled, "It's like a dream come true, Deena. Thank you, Kyle."

"God has been good," he said.

Deena leaned against him, "Yes, Margaret, God has been very good. He gave me a very special husband, a wonderful daughter. . .and now, a son."

Margaret smiled at Orrin. "So much for all that worry. What we needed to do was trust God to work things out."

Deena nodded, "And they did work out, but it wasn't easy."

Stern drew Deena to him. "It certainly wasn't. Trust is a hard lesson to learn, but," he looked down at her, "one well worth the learning." Then he smiled.